Encounters with Anim

SIMON BURT is the au
Peacock and *Just Like Eddie*, and one book of stories, *Floral Street*, all published by Faber & Faber. He attended Downside School and Trinity College, Dublin, and has worked as a teacher, a bookseller and membership secretary of English PEN. He lives in London and is researching a novel based on the life of King Saul.

CHARLOTTE JOHNSON WAHL's 'Young Man Reading' provides an image for the cover of this book. She is represented by Cosa Gallery, Ledbury Mews, London W11. <www.thisiscosa.com>

Encounters with Animals

Simon Burt

STARHAVEN

Contents

ISBN 0-936315-23-7

STARHAVEN, 42 Frognal, London NW3 6AG
in U.S., c/o Box 2573, La Jolla, CA 92038
books@starhaven.org.uk
www.starhaven.org.uk

Typeset in ITC Novarese by John Mallinson
Printed by CPI, 38 Ballard's Lane, London N3 2BJ

in loving memory
of
Eletha Roberts
1922-2005

Encounters with Animals (1)

My friend Ricardo is dying.

My friend Ricardo lives in a hospice, a tall, light building full of air and hope, and I visit him every day.

We sit in his room. We have no choice but to sit in his room. It is not likely that my friend Ricardo will leave his room again. The room has my friend Ricardo's pictures on the walls. Its cupboards bulge with my friend Ricardo's clothes. It is full of books and flowers. And friends.

Friends come and go. There is laughter. The fridge fills up with fruit and wine. We eat and drink. Every day is like a party.

And we sit. I sit in a chair at the foot of the bed. A complicated chair with levers, a chair designed for sick people, a chair my friend Ricardo will never sit in. He is too sick to sit anywhere but on the bed. In the bed. Propped with pillows. His body is worn to a string. His voice is the only thing about him that hasn't changed.

He tells us stories. Stories about ourselves. About visitors who have just left, visitors who will soon be arriving, visitors who are here now, dotted about the room, the room full of people and books and flowers. About the staff. About the nurses. Many of whom during the course of the day will be dotted about the room, talking with the visitors.

We laugh. My friend Ricardo has an enormous laugh. A laugh too big, too loud for a body worn to a string.

Sometimes he sleeps. Often he sleeps. The room is full of people, and he sleeps. While he sleeps, we, the visitors, tell each other stories about ourselves, about each other, so that the party will still be going when he wakes up.

Because, for my friend Ricardo, the room, though full, is empty.

My friend Ricardo is in love.

If my friend Ricardo has a fault, we, the visitors, think – and he has many, we know, we, his visitors, when we meet around the building, when we speak to each other on the telephone, when we meet in the evening in bars, the main topic of conversation is my friend Ricardo's faults – we think he doesn't know how to love.

He loves, as he does everything else, we think, as witness the room full of people, the books and flowers, the fridge full of wine and fruit, greedily.

More, he loves obsessively, we think. Possessively, dominatingly, we think. He loves consumingly. A love that could eat you alive.

And he loves a boy who does not love him. A boy who no longer loves him. A boy who may or may not love him, but is certainly unwilling to be eaten alive.

The burden of my friend Ricardo's love is too great for the boy to bear. He has laid it down. The ceaseless scenes, the weeping, the stream of presents given then taken away, the unremitting insistence that he do every second of the day exactly what my friend Ricardo wants him to do, be what my friend Ricardo wants him to be, and that now, right now, and gratefully, have driven him away.

And so the room is empty.

Full only of people, visitors who, like me, counsel my friend Ricardo to stop it. To give the boy up. To let the boy go. He is a boy, we say. He is only a boy. How can he carry all this?

Let him go, we say.

Yes, we say. Yes, of course. Love him. Keep the love. But let him go. Then at least, if you don't have him, you will have the love.

No, my friend Ricardo says. No. Why should I? I am dying. And he is what I want. Why should I go to my grave without him?

My friend Ricardo, we, the visitors, think, is killing himself. He has used illness, we tell each other, all his life to get what he wants. And now he is dying, to get this boy.

But, we say. But.

No, my friend Ricardo says. No.

But the boy doesn't come.

Every day a party, and the boy doesn't come.

My friend Ricardo has a joint bank account with the boy. He keeps the statements in a leather folder by his bed.

Two years ago, my friend Ricardo sold his flat, paid off some of his debts, and bought a new flat for himself and the boy. And they opened a joint account for the running expenses of the flat.

Because back then the boy did love him. In the beginning. There is no question, we, the visitors, tell each other, that back then the boy loved him. Back then the boy was bowled over by him.

Once, back then, in one of the bars, during a row – the boy was supposed to go with my friend Ricardo to France: they would travel along the Normandy coast eating delicious food and seeing wonderful sights, they would sit long over wine at tables overlooking the sea and life would be sweet, only the boy didn't want to go; it was a great offer, but he saw the strings, even back then, even loving my friend Ricardo, he saw the strings and didn't want to go, and my friend Ricardo said, as he always said if he didn't get what he wanted, If you loved me you'd come, If you don't come it means you don't love me – the boy stood on his chair and made an announcement. He stood on his barstool and he addressed the bar.

I want you all to know, he said, that I love this man. I am

bowled over by this man. I love him, OK? I'm just not going to France with him.

They went to France. They travelled along the Normandy coast, eating delicious food, and seeing wonderful sights. They sat long over wine at tables overlooking the sea. Life was sweet, and when they came back, they moved into my friend Ricardo's flat together.

My friend Ricardo's flat. Full of my friend Ricardo's books and flowers, pictures and clothes. And friends. Never empty of my friend Ricardo's friends. Where he had to do what he was told to do, be what he was told to be, and that now, right now, and gratefully.

He stayed for a week. At the end of that week he went out one morning – it was a Sunday – for the papers, and he didn't come back. My friend Ricardo waited in his flat full of books and flowers, pictures and clothes, and friends, and waited. But the boy didn't come back.

We heard of him, we, the visitors, after that. After that all we did was hear of him.

He's taken up with someone else, we heard. He's telephoned, we heard, and is coming to visit. He's come to visit, but they have quarrelled, and he's gone again.

He's not taken up with someone else, but he's taken a flat somewhere else, in another part of town.

He's going to go to film school. My friend Ricardo is going to help him to get into film school. No, he's not going to go to film school. He may or may not be going to film school, but my friend Ricardo is not going to help him.

Now we no longer hear of him. We hear, that is, of his absence, but not of him.

There was a time when he was going to come to the hospice. We were all warned that he was coming to the hospice, and we would have to make ourselves scarce. We made ourselves scarce, but he didn't come.

Now we all know, even my friend Ricardo knows, that he is not going to come.

So, we say, what are you going to do with the joint account? When are you going to close the joint account? Why don't you close the joint account?

No, my friend Ricardo says. No. It's all of him that I have and I'm going to keep it.

And he keeps the statements in a leather folder by his bed. Sometimes, when we come in, he is holding the leather folder, clasping the leather folder to his chest. Sometimes he spends all day clasping the leather folder to his chest.

Every month a new statement arrives and he adds it to the folder. There is virtually nothing in the account. Since it was opened the boy has made neither deposit nor withdrawal. All the statement records is an amount directly debited to the account from my friend Ricardo's salary.

Now my friend Ricardo has left the room we, the visitors, thought he would never leave. His parents have come and taken him home.

For a while, we, the visitors, hang around the hospice, not knowing what to do. The room is not my friend Ricardo's room any more. It is someone else's room, and we, the visitors, are confined to the public floors, the dining room, the garden. We come to the hospice still. It is still a light, tall building, full of air and hope, and we still need lightness, air and hope. We meet and talk. We laugh. But every day fewer and fewer of us come.

In the end I stop going. I stay at home, and every day I call my friend Ricardo on the telephone. I call his flat and I get his voice on the answering machine. I call his flat to get his voice on the answering machine. Throughout all this his voice is the only thing that hasn't changed.

I keep my friend Ricardo's phone number in my address book.

I keep the address book by my bed. Sometimes I just sit, holding the address book, open at my friend Ricardo's page. Sometimes I clasp it to my chest.

On the day of my friend Ricardo's funeral – he was buried at home, a quiet funeral at home; there was a memorial service at the hospice later to which all of us, the visitors, already beginning not to recognise each other, came, and the boy did not come – but on the day of his funeral I saw the birds.

I was lying on my bed. I was holding my address book, open at my friend Ricardo's page. It was raining, and my lover called me to the kitchen.

Look, he said. Come quick and look at this.

Across from the kitchen window, across balconies and gardens from the kitchen window, is a roof onto which a neighbour throws bread for the pigeons. All day the roof is crowded with pigeons. And today it is raining. Rain is rushing down a drainpipe and out of a spout at the bottom on to the roof, forming a waterfall before it flows away down another pipe. Pigeons are lining up for a shower at the waterfall. First one pigeon, then another, then a third, is standing under the waterspout and shaking and preening in the shower.

The third pigeon lifts its wing and lets the water run under it. Then the other wing. It shakes and moves away and a fourth pigeon takes its place. The remaining pigeons move up the queue.

Look, my lover says. For heaven's sake. Would you look at that.

Daniel Nemo

It is raining. It has been raining for three weeks. Every day for three weeks. It is the wettest March in decades.

It is midnight and it is raining. Across the window fall gurgles and dashes of rain. Swirls and pantings of rain. Daniel is standing at the window looking out at the rain.

I have known Daniel for years. We grew up together, I guess. We went to the same prep school. We were in the same house at Hales. We went to university together. You can call that growing up if you like.

I have known him for years, anyway. I explained to the woman. The woman who asked. The woman who came to the party with him. We go way back, I explained. We meet at parties and places. You can call that knowing someone. You can.

So, she said. The woman said. Tell me about Daniel.

Her name is Jessica.

We are at a gallery opening. A friend of ours from Trinity, now a partner in a firm of Bedford Row lawyers, has opened the partnership's public rooms, hung them with pictures, and flung a party. All the partners and all the painters have been asked to invite all their friends. The rooms are crowded and as hot as a midden. Daniel and Jessica and I are packed up against a wall at the end of the farthest room. I have just returned his greeting.

Hi, Daniel, I have said. Long time no see. How are you? How's the house?

When I last saw Daniel he had just bought a house. A three-storeyed house in Parson's Green, which he was doing up himself. Slowly. Fitfully. Money was scarce.

Hi, Daniel has said. Fine. The roof leaks. The roof leaks quite a bit. I can't afford to do much about it. This is Jessica.

So, Jessica says.

She is, I see, young. Younger than Daniel and I anyway. Quite young then. Ten years younger.

Tell me about Daniel, she says.

Oh Daniel, I say. Daniel and I go way back. Daniel and I grew up together. We went to the same prep school. We were in the same house at Hales. We went to Trinity together. We go way back.

They have been, I see, quarrelling. Or Jessica has been trying to quarrel. It is not easy to quarrel with Daniel. He subtracts himself.

Jessica, I see, is angry. It is easy to be angry with Daniel. He subtracts himself. I cannot remember the number of conversations I have had with people who were angry with Daniel.

Yes, she says. No doubt. But what was he like?

Daniel is standing next to me, against the wall. Jessica is facing us, her back to the room. Daniel appears to be looking over her shoulder. He has subtracted himself. Waiters and office juniors are circulating with bottles of wine. Plates of sandwiches. Jugs of Guinness.

Well, I say. You know. I didn't know him so well.

At All Hallows, you understand, I say, all alliances were defensive. We used to play games together. Rugby. I scored a try once. After he tackled me. We scrambled and I scored a try. He left a year before I did. A year was a long time at Hales. We read different things at Trinity. He was like he is now, I guess.

He was. He was just the same. He had the same gift then of being there and not there at the same time. I am used to it. Jessica, clearly, not.

Was he always beautiful? she says.

Oh yes, I say. Beautiful. He was always beautiful.

His beauty was the first thing you noticed about Daniel. Often you noticed nothing else. Often you could notice nothing else. Daniel's beauty hit you like a club. Even now, even after growing up together, even after twenty five years, it could stop your breath. Daniel's beauty.

Oh yes, I say. Oh yes. Beautiful. He was always beautiful.

She laughs. It is not a pleasant laugh.

Daniel stops a passing waiter or office junior and we replenish our glasses.

I sometimes think, Jessica says, that he hasn't got anything else. I think it quite often, actually. I'm thinking it right now. Actually.

We used to call him Nemo, I say. At All Hallows. After Captain Nemo.

I glance across at Daniel. He is deep in his Guinness. It is possible, I think, that he remembers the same things that I do. It is equally possible that he does not. It is also possible that he is not listening.

We called him Captain Nemo because of his expression. This expression he sometimes had. This distant, vacant expression. The lights were on, his expression said, but there was no one at home. There were times when Daniel looked so dull-eyed and empty you would have sworn he had no brain. It is possible that this expression was not a true reflection of his state of mind. It is possible that this expression, like his beauty, was an accident of physiognomy only. We never asked. We called him Captain Nemo, and we left him alone.

The name stuck to him. Later, after Trinity, when we were closer, he told me that he had never been unhappy with it. The one thing he knew he wanted to do, he said, when he was ready, was to submerge like Captain Nemo, and have his life to himself. The only difficulty, he said, was knowing when he was ready. When he had enough provisions to submerge with.

I glance at Jessica and see her glancing at Daniel. He is

looking over her shoulder at the crowd. It is probably in response to this probable detachment that she asks her next question.

And love, she says. What about love? Since you know him so well. Has he ever been in love?

Oh, I say. Love. I don't know about love.

Nothing bored Daniel more than his beauty. It was, he told me, after Trinity, when we were closer, nothing but boring. It is boring, he told me, that people should think that you are turning the melting batteries of your eyes on them when you are merely looking at them.

We were drinking together, I remember, in a Soho club, and I was telling him that we were not going to be close any more. I was telling him that it simply isn't possible to be close to someone who most of the time simply isn't there. And I caught him looking with what looked like bleak and brimming eyes into the middle distance.

Don't look so sad, I said. It isn't so sad.

Oh, he said, refocusing his eyes on me, I'm not sad. I'm just looking at the teletext over the bar.

You can, after all, if you like, attribute moral qualities to beauty. You can extrapolate a fine nose into a fine spirit. A pencilled brow into a lofty spirit. A pensive mien into a delicate spirit. You can. If you like.

Oh, I say. Love.

And I laugh. My laugh, I imagine, is as pleasant to Jessica's ears as Jessica's was to mine.

A waiter or office junior hovers and we again replenish our glasses.

Love and Daniel, I say, are mutually exclusive concepts.

Not true. Not wholly true.

Over the years, I know, many people have loved Daniel, and have been deluded by his beauty, his beauty and his careless generosity with it, into thinking first that he loved them, second that he was incapable of loving. Them or anyone.

Close, but not wholly true.

Daniel loves books. All the time I have known him Daniel has loved books.

At All Hallows the library covered three long walls with tall floor-to-ceiling bookcases, and you could always find Daniel hanging from them. When he left many of the books left with him.

At Hales barely a weekend passed without Daniel's taking the train to Bath and returning with cherished volumes. He specialised in the uniform or collected editions you could buy then. Hardbacks only. Lawrence, Hardy, Conrad, Faulkner, Virginia Woolf. I would visit him in his room when he got back to see what he had bought. He would take a book from the shelf, open it, hold it up to his face, and inhale its deep fragrance.

At Trinity, where neither of us had much money, he would haunt the bookshops, buying paperbacks now, stealing where he couldn't buy. He would order nothing. He would read nothing in libraries. It was part of the task he set himself that he had to come across the books he wanted by chance only, and possess them.

After Trinity, when he used only second hand shops, he applied the same rule, buying only what he found. Book search was a luxury he didn't allow.

His father, he told me later, when we were closer, had been a designer. He designed book covers. And when Daniel was young the only books that were in the house were the books for which his father had designed the cover. This element of accident was, he said, part of the point.

He insisted, too, on the complete works of his chosen writers. Despite the strictures of chance he had built up an immense collection. He had a complete Landor, the Welby and Wheeler edition, assembled from randomly discovered volumes. He had the Cook and Wedderburn Ruskin, ditto. The Masson de Quincy, ditto. The Howe Hazlitt, ditto. The Harold Williams Swift, the Cunningham Walpole, ditto. He had rooms full of books.

No one, I think, who has seen Daniel with his books would say that he is incapable of love. He spends hours at his shelves. He moves lingeringly from volume to volume. He chooses a book at random to read over breakfast, and within minutes is chasing themes and references through shelf after shelf. And you can call that love. You can.

Jessica, I assume, has not seen Daniel among his books.

Because, Yes, she says. Oh yes. You can say that again.

She waves down a passing waiter or office junior and replenishes her glass again.

Oh yes, she says. You can say that again.

The waiter or office junior offers the Guinness jug to Daniel and to me. We both decline.

This seems more than Jessica can bear. She draws a sharp breath and darts Daniel a look of fury. She bends down and puts her glass on the floor.

Well, she says, when she is upright again. It's been lovely. But it's a bit hot for me.

She opens her handbag and looks into it. She closes it again.

I think, she says, I'll leave you two to your reunion.

And she turns and walks away.

Daniel and I stay where we are. I lean against the wall. Daniel, I see, follows Jessica with his eyes as she pushes through the crowd to the door and away. When she has gone he leans against the wall next to me.

Sorry about that, he says.

I smile.

I should have seen it coming, I guess, I say.

Yes, he says. So should I. I guess.

We lean against the wall without saying anything. The crowd, held back before by Jessica, pushes into us. As we lean against the wall I feel Daniel's hand move down my arm till it meets mine and holds it.

It is clear enough, I think, what he is offering.

Come to that, I think, it is clear enough what I am offering too.

Which brings me to where we started.

To me, that is, waking up, sitting up, in bed, at midnight. To the wettest March in years. To the windows dashed with rain, and to Daniel standing naked at them. To Daniel's body dappled by reflected rain, peach coloured in the street light. To Daniel's eyes bleak and brimming in the halogen light.

It is possible I think that he is thinking the same thing that I am. It is equally possible that he is not.

I sit up further against the pillows.

What? I say. What?

Daniel looks out at the rain.

It is possible, I think, that he is thinking of his books. Of his books and his leaking roof. Of the rain trickling and washing through his leaking roof and down over his books, down over paper, leather and board, soaking into and swelling paper and leather and board, melting away paper, leather and board.

Daniel says something out over the rain.

What? I say. What?

Can we stop now, please? he says.

The Clock

The next day we went on this outing. At breakfast Ted said let's go on this outing. We could call Stan and Renee, they'll come too. We'll go to Salisbury, look around, have a meal, make a day of it.

I've always hated outings. I mean, all you do is go to places. I live in a place, right? Salisbury's just a place, right? I mean, why just change places.

We've got stale, Ted said. We don't do anything. The way we used to. We used to go out. We don't go out any more.

I didn't say anything. I didn't want to go. What's in Salisbury that I haven't got at home?

Come on, Joanie, Ted said. Don't take it so hard. Don't take it so personally. It's just one of those things. Come on. We'll go out for the day. Take your mind off.

You're meant to have fun on outings. Other people have fun on outings. Ted and Stan and Renee have fun on outings. I just trail around. They do daft things. They sit on the pavement and eat ice cream. I just smile and hang around till it's time to go home. I'd rather stay home.

Ted phoned Stan and Renee and we went to Salisbury. It took two and a half hours to get there. We parked in the market place and looked round the shops. It was a hot, hot day. We poked around the streets.

What a pretty town, Ted kept on saying. What a pretty town. Joanie, wouldn't you like to live in a town like this?

We had lunch in this old hotel, just off the market place.

We ought to see Stonehenge, Renee said. Now we're here.

We can't come all this way and not see Stonehenge.

There's the cathedral too, Ted said. We've got to see the cathedral.

We went to Stonehenge after lunch. I fell asleep in the car on the way there. When we arrived, Ted and Stan and Renee went off to look at the stones. I stayed in the car and slept a bit more. It really was hot.

Then we drove back to Salisbury and parked in the market square again and went to look at the cathedral.

It was cool inside the cathedral. It was full of light and air and dead people.

They've got Magna Carta in here, Stan said. We ought to look at Magna Carta.

We walked around a bit. Renee had steel tips on her heels and they clattered.

Stan kept shushing her and telling her she was too fat, she walked too heavily. In the end she took her shoes off.

You can't take your shoes off in church, Stan said.

Can't I though? Renee said. What do you care about church? First time you've seen the inside of one in years.

In one of the aisles of the cathedral they've got this clock. It isn't a clock really. Just the works. It's big. A big, square metal frame with cogs and weights and things, and a huge, long loop of rope that goes way up into the roof to move the hands on the clock in the tower.

I sat down to look at the clock.

Come on, Joanie, they all said. We're going to look at Magna Carta.

You go, I said. I'm going to stay here for a bit.

No matter how hard I looked I couldn't see the rope move. It was a wide open sort of machine. Just a few simple pieces of moving metal. Thunk, thunk, thunk, it went. Thunk, thunk, thunk.

Then Ted came back and sat next to me and put his arm

round my shoulder.

All right, Joanie? he said. How's my Joanie?

Then Stan and Renee came back.

All right? Stan said.

Joanie's all right, Ted said. Aren't you, Joanie?

I've had an idea, Stan said. Why don't we stay over? We could have dinner at that hotel. And stay the night. And go on home tomorrow.

I'm game, Ted said. Good idea, eh, Joanie? Make a night of it.

We haven't got any things, I said.

Good old Joanie, Stan said. Always the practical one. Tell you what. You and Renee go and buy toothbrushes and things. And Ted and I will go and book a room.

All the time Renee and I were in the shops I kept on hoping. Maybe there wouldn't be any room at the hotel, or it would be too expensive or something.

We just bought toothbrushes. Renee didn't think we'd need anything else.

Ted and Stan had booked rooms by the time we got there. We had tea and sandwiches and cream cakes and went and walked round the town again. Renee bought a new dress and a pair of summer shoes.

Stan got fresh with Renee over dinner. He kept on grabbing her leg and putting his hand up her skirt under the table.

Stan, she said. Stop it, Stan. People will see.

I can't help it, Stan said. It's the hotel. I always get randy in hotels. Just wait till I get you upstairs, eh?

It was a big dinner with wine and things. We had liqueurs afterwards. Renee got the giggles and Stan took her up to bed.

Soon after that Ted and I went up too. I got straight into bed and curled up. Then Ted got in and pulled me round to face him. He cuddled up close. I could feel his limp, damp thing flop against my hand. My head got buried between his neck and the pillow and I couldn't breathe very well.

There, there, he said. My Joanie. Night night, Joanie.

He kissed me and turned over. Soon he was asleep. I lay there thinking.

What I don't understand, I thought, is why it's always the same. They way people woo you gently, gently, gently out of your shell, and then step on you. That's what I don't understand.

I couldn't sleep. I thought of the clock. That big, old clock. That was some clock. That clock was really something.

Two Foccacias and a Rye

We had to introduce ourselves. There were sixteen of us. All women. The place was a dump. A classroom. Dusty. Dirty. Muddy lino on the floor. I decided not to mind.

Very hot. A blazing day outside. But if you opened the window even a crack there was a bellow of noise from the street. Window open, you were deafened. Window shut, you boiled. There were sixteen of us. We all arrived separately. The windows went up and down sixteen times.

When the tutor arrived, I don't know why, but I expected sandals. I had a very clear picture. A horse face, a black pullover, a tartan skirt, sandals. And a warm manner. What we got was Come Dancing. The Smile. The Posture. A grey wool dress. Rather good. Hair swept back into a loose bun. The accent north country, but very, very polished. You could see the tendons in her throat tighten as she spoke. GID moaning, E-verone, she said. I'm Ing-rid. I decided not to mind.

And we had to introduce ourselves. We had to go round the room, saying our name and the adjective we thought best described us. I'll start, Ing-rid said. I'm Indistrious Ing-rid. That is what she said. Indistrious.

A mistake that, I think. Not only, as we soon discovered, was it not the best adjective. Inefficient Ing-rid would have been entirely more appropriate. We never began a session without at least a minute's, well, dithering. Now, where were we? What were we doing last? But the alliteration was a mistake too. As we went round the room, we vied with each other to be alliterative.

There was Lustrous Lucy. There was Bubbly Barbara. There was Cool Caroline, Generous Jennifer and Wonderful Winnie. There was Angry Andrea, which I rather liked, until it became obvious that it was the simple truth. There was Harrassed Henrietta and Practical Pauline and Laughing Lisa. One almost expected a Hard-hearted Hannah. I decided to mind.

My husband always used to call me Irritable Isobel. Don't, he would say, be such an irritable Isobel. Isobel is my second name. I never liked it. It was my mother's name. I decided to mind so much that I nearly used it. In the end I used Jane. GID moaning, e-ver-y-one, I said. I'm Jaundiced Jane. Another mistake.

Because it wasn't simply an ice breaker. You know the sort of thing. It has always bored me. It was A Mnemonic. We had to go round the room again, naming everyone from memory. Lustrous Lucy, Cool Caroline, Laughing Lisa, Bubbly Barbara. By the time it came to my turn I had heard Jaundiced Jane eight times. I heard it seven more. I regretted it by the second time. And from now on, Indistrious Ing-rid went on to say, whenever we met, we were to greet each other by name and adjective. Generous Jennifer, Wonderful Winnie, Good morning. Hi there, Jaundiced Jane. It got less formal as the term went on. I ended up as Jaundiced Janey.

After a while I made some friends. Course friends. We sat next to each other in class. Generous Jennifer, Wonderful Winnie, and me. Generous Jennifer was a masseuse. Wonderful Winnie was an actress. Had been an actress. What she did now was belly dance in pubs. Neither had any children. Neither was married. Wonderful Winnie had had a husband, but he disappeared. Generous Jennifer had what she called a partner. A Dane. He spent much of his time in Denmark. The best place for him, Generous Jenny said.

One more thing I decided to mind. We had to go round the room yet again. And this time we had to say our name, and one good thing that had happened to us. In the course of, say, the last year.

I noticed it straightaway: Hello everyone, I'm Musical Margaret, and the good thing that's happened to me is that my daughter has got into art school. I'm Laughing Lisa, and the good thing that's happened to me is that my husband has got a very good new job. I'm Bubbly Barbara, and the good thing that's happened to me is that I thought my lover was on drugs, and he isn't. It was ridiculous, I thought. Ridiculous and sad. All these women, and the one good thing that's happened to them in a year is something that's happened to someone else.

I mean, I have a daughter. Phoebe. Phoebe after the moon. Because when she was a baby she had a big, round, moon face. But I'm not going to be ridiculous about it. And this was supposed to be something that had happened to me.

The only trouble was, I couldn't think of anything that had happened to me. Like Angry Andrea. Hi, I'm Angry Andrea, and I can't think of one good thing that's happened to me. We all laughed. When it came to my turn I said, Hello. I'm Jaundiced Jane. And the good thing that's happened to me is I've decided to come on this course.

Phoebe lives here with me. We get on well. We talk. At the end of the day she tells me what she's done at school, and I tell her what I've done on the course. She laughed at Indistrious Ing-rid and Angry Andrea. She called herself Furious Phoebe. We laughed at that.

Her moon face, like her father, is long gone. She grew out of it. She's slim now, with high cheek bones. Like her father's. A high nose. Like her father's. Sometimes, when I look up suddenly, it could be her father.

Then we had to divide up. Into groups of three. And talk about A Topic. We were to remember A Moment when we felt Utterly Powerless. Otterly powerless. A Moment when there was Just Nothing We Could Do. I chose the music from next door.

The neighbours here are difficult. They play music very loud. They used to play it. My group was Generous Jennifer and Wonderful Winnie. Wonderful Winnie talked about how she had been mugged. How someone had run up behind her one night and hit her over the head with a bottle. Generous Jennifer talked about how she gets a panic attack whenever she gets a letter from the Bank.

The neighbours are Italian. They moved in about a year ago. The first thing they did was throw a party. Yelling and singing and unbelievable music until God knows when in the morning. I telephoned. I went round and tried to reason with them. I even called the police. It was right next to my bedroom. It was like being in the same room.

And it didn't stop there. They liked their music. You never knew when it was going to start. It started one day at lunchtime, and when I knocked on the door two hours later there was no one in. They have a shop on the ground floor, a delicatessen. I asked there, and some toothless Nonna behind the counter told me they'd gone out to Il Cas' An' Carry. They'd just left the music on.

It went on for months. It made Phoebe cry. One night. Two or three in the morning. Music bouncing off the walls. It made Phoebe cry and cry. I have never felt more Otterly Powerless. Everyone told me afterwards that I wasn't. That I could stop it. You can go to the Environmental Health, Laughing Lisa said, and get it stopped. I know, I said. I know now.

Laughing Lisa made Phoebe laugh. What made Laughing Lisa feel powerless. She was walking down the street one day, and there was a boy walking in front of her. A Teenager. With a couple of girls. He was cramming Chewits into his mouth, and just chucking the paper on to the street. And Laughing Lisa knew that there was nothing she could do. It made her so angry. But she could just imagine what a Teenager would say to some bossy old woman who asked him to pick his sweet papers up. We laughed at that.

You've seen the graffiti, of course. The graffito. The Fuck You. It moves. It appeared a month or two ago. I had it painted out. It appeared again the next day, and I had it painted out again. I have it regularly painted out. And it's regularly painted back.

I can't think why. I mean, I can't think who would want to do it, can you? I said to the police, it's not as if I've offended anyone. It's not as if I've been involved in a lengthy quarrel with anyone, or anything. One thing I have learned. In matters of this sort the police are absolutely useless.

They made no attempt to help me with the music. None. And with the graffiti all they say is that they need to know who does it before they can do anything. Well, of course they do. What I don't understand is why they don't. A careful watch on the wall and there you are, I would have thought. Manpower, they say. Important though your wall is, they say, we cannot spare the manpower to spend a whole night watching it.

It was not the first graffito. The first one came just after they arrived. The neighbours. They had been here a day or two. And Phoebe woke up to see the words Good Morning Phoebe, spray-painted on to the wall opposite her window.

We are a cul-de-sac here. In Neville Place. We are a row of buildings that used to be shops. Some of us still are. You can see the street is not very wide. More of a lane really. The wall is the wall of the garden of Neville House.

When we moved here it was all very run down. Just a row of grubby old shops. A grocer, a cobbler, a pet shop. We bought this place and converted it. And soon other people came, and did the same thing. We turned the old shop into a dining room. Other people kept it. There is a flower shop, a china shop, a poetry bookshop, a pottery gallery, an antique shop.

It's rather pretty. And now it has graffiti. And an Italian delicatessen.

They have spoken, the police say, to the neighbours. Their name is Angeli. The Angelis, the police say, think that it's us. I can see it, I say. Can't you? My eight year old daughter and me. Out with a spray can in the middle of the night.

There is a son. Angelo, his name is. The first graffito, I know, was written by him. He is ten years old. I found him talking with Phoebe on the street the day after the party. He goes to the same school. A little place in Holland Park. I put a stop to it. I don't think it's wise, I said. Do you? And the next day there it was. Good Morning Phoebe. Letters a foot high. And I'm supposed not to know who is doing it.

Anyway, the course. It's a Counselling course. Co-counselling. I felt I ought to do something. In fact, it isn't as simple as you might think. A large part of it is what Indistrious Ing-rid, with her genteel vowels, calls Rule Play. You work with your group. One to speak. One to listen. The third to Offer Comment. It's surprisingly difficult.

Sometimes, Indistrious Ing-rid does a display session. She asks for a volunteer, and plays the part of listener while the volunteer talks. The rest of us Offer Comment. This alone would ensure that I never volunteered. I'm sorry, I decided to say, but I think you ought to know. I don't do Rule Play.

Until I was asked. When I was asked I got up meekly enough. I sat next to Indistrious Ing-rid, and before I knew it I was simply gabbling. About my husband. My ex-husband. About how he wanted a baby and I didn't. I hadn't enjoyed being a child. Childhood is not something I would wish on anyone.

But he wanted one, so we tried. It can make you feel decidedly odd, all that trying. Like a brood mare. A tupped ewe. We went to doctors. We underwent tests. It was no one's fault, they said. It was just taking a long time to take. It took in the end. I was eight months pregnant. Hauling myself about. Uddered like a milch cow. Varicose in every vein. And he left. I woke up one morning and he hadn't come home. He was a barrister. He sent a letter. I could have whatever I wanted. The house. All sorts of money. Anything.

He had been seeing someone else. All that time we were trying for Phoebe. He came to the hospital. To see Phoebe. He said I should call her Phoebe. And I agreed, because it simply didn't occur to me that he wasn't coming back. That Someone Else was downstairs in the car. That he was coming to say goodbye.

I don't know why he did it. I mean I know why he did it. It happens all the time. But all that about the baby. All those tests and tupped ewe sessions. For a baby he wasn't going to stay for. For a child he knew I didn't want. Not really want it. That's what I said. Sitting opposite Indistrious Ing-rid. With her smile. Afterwards everyone Offered Comment. I didn't hear. I was busy with the Kleenex. Indistrious Ing-rid, with her Come Dancing vowels.

And then it was homework time. Think of something you have done which was Crowned With Soccess. I talked it over with Phoebe. I enjoy doing homework with Phoebe. We do hers and then we do mine.

It wasn't easy. Eventually I came up with an idea. How I stopped the noise. How I put the Environmental Health on to them. It took a long time, but we got them in the end. They were fined. Five hundred pounds. Since then we have had comparative peace. An Effort Crowned with Soccess. And we're not supposed to know who is scrawling obscenities on our wall.

Phoebe wasn't as helpful as usual, actually. She was almost angry. She thought all that was over, she said.

It is, I said. It's only for the course. I said. It's only a course, I said.

A tirade last night from Angry Andrea. About the lottery, of all things. The lottery and the English. Laughing Lisa doesn't approve of the lottery. She has seen many people ruined by gambling, she says, and she can't approve.

I was going to say I quite liked it. I was going to say it gives people two seconds of pleasure. Once when they buy their ticket. And again just before the draw, when they think they might win. But Angry Andrea jumped in. Angry Andrea, have I said? is American. She doesn't like the English. The English, she says, are frumpish, snobbish, middle-brow and mean. And she thinks the lottery is guaranteed to Clean Up in England. Because there is nothing the English love more than carping at success, and here it is, a spectacular success every week to carp at. Laughing Lisa was livid. I don't know why I'm telling you this.

A tirade this morning from Furious Phoebe. About coming home from school. She has never liked her school. She has never liked school. Even her first school, playgroup across the park in Neville Crescent. Morning after morning, sulks, headaches, tears. Once she ran away. I got a phone call from her grandmother, saying Phoebe was with her. She had walked out of playgroup and taken a bus down to her in Markham Square.

She loved her grandmother. Her grandmother was not a loveable woman. She was never, she would have been the first to admit, a loveable woman. But Phoebe loved her.

She has been to several schools, and she hasn't liked any of them. She especially hasn't liked her present one. Until recently. Which was what was behind the tirade, of course. All I said was I wanted to be sure she came straight home. And she screamed at me. Why shouldn't she stay if she wants? Why can't she take as long to come home as she wants? Other children take as long to come home as they want. I didn't say anything.

It's the Angelis, of course. Angelo Angeli, the sprig of the Delicatessen. And I'm not having it. They walk home together. They sit and chat in some coffee place in the High Street. I can't have that.

Homework was to talk about a failure. Something you put Heart and Soul of Effort into, and it didn't work. I didn't discuss it with Phoebe. Not after the tirade. This I did all on my own. That damned little boy.

Because Phoebe is a name for the moon. Little Angelo looked it up in the Classical Dictionary. In the library, one imagines. I can't see the Angelis having one. And Phoebe, he discovered, was the name of the old goddess of the moon. Her granddaughter, the new goddess, defeated and replaced her, and took the name. Something like that. She was, in effect, her own granddaughter. Two little children in a coffee bar. Talking about Greek mythology. The finer points, wouldn't you say? of Greek mythology. I think I can be forgiven for not expecting that.

The upshot was that Phoebe wanted to know about her grandmother. I don't remember her, she said. Her grandmother died when she was four. A matter of weeks, in fact, after Phoebe ran away from playgroup. She had cancer. Of the throat. She had a voice box. It sounded like she was talking to you over the phone even when she wasn't. Phoebe didn't mind. But she died. And Phoebe forgot her. Children forget. Until little Angelo reminded her.

My mother was my homework. All the time, all those years, I spent trying to make her like me. She simply didn't. She never did. It wasn't my fault, she said. It wasn't anything to do with me. I wasn't alone. She didn't like most people.

It should have been sad really. She told her nurse. You can imagine, she had umpteen nurses. They wouldn't stay. She told this one anyway that she didn't mean to be the way she was. She didn't like being that way. She just couldn't help it. Sometimes she could hear herself, she said, opening her mouth and all this poison pouring out.

Once, when I was young, when I was Phoebe's age, I was walking home through the village, and a car came racing round the corner and knocked me into the hedge. I wasn't hurt. Bumps and bruises. Frightened. I was sent to hospital though, for a few days, just in case, and the driver came to visit me with a bunch of flowers and a huge box of chocolates. What a charming man, my mother said, to come and see her like that. He must have known she was upset. Such lovely flowers. She couldn't wait to get home and put them in water. And however did he know these were her favourite chocolates?

When she found out she had cancer, she was living in South Africa. I flew out to see her. I thought, at last there is something I can do. It was no good. I'm going home, she said. I've taken a house in Markham Square. I've booked a nurse. There was really no need for you to come all this way.

But Phoebe loved her. And she loved Phoebe. It wasn't easy, watching her love Phoebe. Phoebe wasn't frightened by the voicebox. She and Phoebe would laugh at the voicebox. Oh Granny, you do sound funny. Yes, darling, I sound like a Dalek, don't I? She never called me Darling. Not once.

I couldn't have him bringing up all that. I put my foot down. The only trouble is, she won't listen. I know she's still seeing him. And what am I supposed to do? Time for the nuns, I thought. Right in the middle of the tirade, I thought it's time for the nuns. I leave you to imagine what they said on the course about the nuns. But I didn't budge. Nothing wrong with nuns. I liked my nuns.

Furious Phoebe. What has she got to be furious about? That's what I'd like to know.

Two seconds of happiness a week. Imagine.

28

A simple homework this week. A Light-hearted One. Nothing to be taken too seriously. It's the end of term, and the last session wasn't going to be a class really. She wanted, Indistrious Ing-rid said, everyone to bring along a Little Something, and we'd have a party. And the homework, too, would be something light, something to bring to a party. An example of something that had happened to us that we didn't understand. It didn't matter what it was. Just as long as we didn't understand it.

Hours of anxious colloquy after class about the theme of the party. Frayed tempers in the canteen. But eventually we decided – Generous Jenny decided, it was all she could afford, she said – on Italian. We all volunteered to bring along something especially Italian. Salami, sun dried tomatoes, olives. I chose bread. I have to say that I forgot. I've had a lot to think about and I forgot. Until I was setting out for class, and running over the reasons I was going to give for not doing my homework, and the only thing I could do, if I wasn't going to be late, was go next door to the Angeli's.

It gave me real trouble, that homework. I simply didn't know what to use. It wasn't as if there was a dearth of things. I mean, my life was full of things I didn't understand. It's just that they didn't fall, it seemed to me, under the heading of Light. And the one thing I really didn't understand, I mean the one thing I totally and absolutely didn't understand, well, I wasn't going to mention that.

All this is because of the little Angeli. Phoebe and the little Angeli. She was always late. It didn't matter what I said, I couldn't stop her being late. She was with him, of course. And one day she was later than usual, and I was doing some tidying. She is not a tidy child, and the only way I can cope with this, because I am tidy, is to have this big cardboard box, and anything of hers left lying around, I pick it up and put it in. If it's still in the box at the end of the week, it goes out. It strikes me as fair.

And this evening, as I was tidying, picking up her clothes and things, her paper and pencils and books, and putting them in the box, I saw something. At the bottom of the box. Clever really, if you think about it. If there is one place in the house I am not likely to look it's in the box. Everything left lying around gets tossed into it. Why would I bother to look through it? And at the bottom of the box I found what I don't understand. What I shall never understand. What would have made up my mind, even if I hadn't found out about all those visits to the coffee bar, that she was going, really going, to the nuns.

How I didn't say anything I shall never know. How I didn't wring her neck I shall never know. You've seen the Fuck Off, of course. The Fuck Offs. I can't clean them off any more. I found. In her box. Hidden away at the bottom of her box. A canister. Of Aerosol paint. It took me a long time to realise what it was for. You can see why I wouldn't want to use it for homework, can't you? Too many Kleenex, quite frankly. Don't you think?

Under normal circumstances, of course, I wouldn't have used the Angelis'. But I was in a hurry. The place was packed. A full complement of Angelis behind the counter. Toothless Nonna at the till. I don't know what I expected. A sudden silence, maybe, when I came in. Awkwardness. Atmosphere. No one seemed to notice. I simply joined the queue, and the business of the shop went on exactly as if I hadn't just had them fined five hundred pounds.

I felt a bit awkward, I have to say. All the more so because I trod on someone's foot in the queue. It was really very crowded. By the time I arrived at the counter I was, I admit it, flustered. I knew I shouldn't have come. I knew I should have stopped off in South Kensington somewhere, and simply been late. When I finally got to the counter, and it was Mr Angeli serving me, last seen in court, I had trouble getting my order out. I asked for two focaccias and a rye.

He looked at me. He didn't understand. Eh? he said. Two focaccias and a rye, I said. He laughed. You hear that? he said. He called out. He asked round the shop. You hear that? This lady, she want two focaccias and a rye.

It sussurated round the shop. Two focaccias and a rye. Two focaccias and a rye. Everybody laughed. All round the shop, laughter. Yes, I said. Two focaccias and a rye. You know, Mr Angeli said, that's funny. That's very funny. You are a funny lady. I had no idea what he meant. But at least, I thought, as I left, I have my homework.

I tried it out in the car on the way to class. Two focaccias and a rye. I couldn't see why it was funny. But it seemed a lighter hearted story somehow, than Furious Phoebe and the aerosol. Don't you think?

Don't you think?

Good Fortune

Missing the train didn't help.

His German, needless to say, was not up to much. So he listened very carefully to the man at the ticket office – Der Beamte, ein Beamter, a verbal noun – when he told him when and from what platform the connection to Mannheim left. He made him repeat it. In German and in English, because he still had trouble with the twenty four hour clock, to make doubly sure.

He hated stations. He felt even lonelier than usual in stations. Stations and laundrettes. He went out of his way to avoid them. What room in his large and very heavy suitcases was not taken up with books was filled with dirty clothes.

The train left from Platform Four at nine thirty two. When he got to the platform there was a train already there. A cross, by the looks of it, between a goods train and a cattle truck. He sat and read – *The Unquiet Grave*, by Palinurus – and waited for it to leave.

He should have known.

He waited and waited, but the goods train showed no sign of leaving. Eventually he got up and went to the ticket office and said, Look. Are you sure you've got it right? There's this goods train on my platform. I've got to get to Mannheim in time for the express.

Yes, they said. That's right. That's the nine thirty two to Mannheim.

The goods train, he said.

That's right, they said. There's a passenger compartment

at the front. Hadn't he seen?

So he went, as fast as his heavy luggage would allow him – that was one of the things he hated about stations: he was terrified all the time that someone was going to steal his luggage; he had to cart it about with him – back to the platform, but the train had gone.

He panicked of course.

He just stood there. He didn't know how long for.

Then he went back to the ticket office and told them what had happened.

Not to worry, they said. There was tram stop round the corner. The tram would get him there in plenty of time.

So he went to the tram stop.

The tram, when it arrived, was full. There was just enough room for him to stand in the aisle with his luggage between his legs.

The journey was maddeningly slow. Most of it he spent muttering, Come on, come on, between his teeth, and jerking his body forward as if to add its impetus to the tram's.

Not sensible, but by this time he was barely in control.

On the outskirts of Mannheim he got a seat. He hooked his legs over his cases and chewed the skin round his fingernails. The tram seemed to stop every hundred yards. Eventually they stopped at the station, and he ran to the enquiry counter.

It wasn't easy to run with half a hundredweight in either hand.

The express, they said, was at Platform Seven. But hurry. It's about to leave.

Hurry!

They could not, he supposed, have looked too closely at him. He was dripping with sweat. his face must have been scarlet.

He hurried.

But it didn't do any good. He arrived at Platform Seven in

time to see the express leave. He watched the tail lights disappear up the track. He felt pretty bloody awful.

He sat on his cases and damn near cried. It was half past twelve at night, and all he had in his pocket was his ticket home, five pounds in English money, and about forty marks.

And *The Unquiet Grave*. Not ideal reading for desperate circumstances, which is what he felt his circumstances were.

Maybe he did cry a bit.

The next time he looked at his watch it was one o'clock. The station was nearly empty. He went back to the enquiry desk, but it was closed. He found a timetable, and worked out that the next train for Ostend was at eleven o'clock the next morning. It had been hard enough to reserve a seat on the train he had missed. He'd probably have to stand half way across Europe.

The left luggage office was closed, and there was a sign on the lockers that said facilities had been suspended until further notice, owing to terrorist activity. Which meant that he would have to stay awake all night to guard his cases. He had slept little the night before and was tired. Not that he could see himself getting much sleep stretched out on a bench, which seemed to be the only recourse left open to him, but it would have been nice to have the option.

The cafeteria was closed.

The waiting room was dark, and he couldn't find the light, and it smelled of beer and vomit anyway.

There didn't seem to be anything else to do. He picked up his cases, which got heavier by the minute, and walked out into the town.

About a hundred yards down the street – he had switched his suitcases from hand to hand twice already – he found a café that was still open.

It didn't look the cleanest place in the world, but he couldn't think of anything else to do but go in and blow some of his marks on a coffee.

There were four or five people sitting here and there about the room, and they seemed no cleaner than the café. He bought a coffee and sat in a corner.

No one looked at him.

No one said anything.

He took out *The Unquiet Grave* and began to read, but he couldn't concentrate, so he sat and stirred his coffee. He drew lines and circles on the froth with his spoon. He felt very sleepy. Every now and then he took a sip. He had all night and couldn't afford many coffees.

He was nodding over the dregs of his second cup when the door opened and a woman came in. He looked up as she passed, but their eyes met and she smiled, so he looked quickly down again. He reopened *The Unquiet Grave*. The next thing he knew she was standing at his table holding two cups of coffee.

Entropy, she said. Coffee gets cold. You look as if you need another one.

She put the cup down in front of him, and pulled out the chair opposite his.

May I? she said.

He nodded, and closed *The Unquiet Grave*.

She put her coffee on the table and moved his two empty cups to the edge. She sat down and offered him a cigarette. He didn't smoke, but he took it. It seemed easier.

So, she said.

So. What brings you to this place?

He could, he felt, have asked the same of her. She looked more out of place than he did. He was wearing his old duffel coat. He was dirty and unkempt. She looked as if she had just stepped out of Harrod's, or whatever the Mannheim equivalent was. Headscarf. Burberry mackintosh. Tweeds. Pearls. About forty to forty five, he guessed. Slightly horsy about the hip and jaw. Carefully waved greying hair.

She smiled.

What is your name? she said.

McHale, he said. J J McHale. I've come from Heidelberg. I've missed the train.

J J, she said. What do they stand for?

I call myself J J, he said. They stand for Julian and Justin.

I can see why you wouldn't use them, she said.

He stirred his coffee. She held her cup to her lips, but didn't drink.

So, J J, she said. Why Heidelberg?

That was not an easy question.

Mainly because he himself was none too clear about the reason.

Like almost everything else he did it was more or less an accident. The result of someone else's decision.

He was not good at deciding what to do. He had left school because he was the right age to leave school. He had got all the necessary A levels because he had been unable to think of anything else to do but work for them. He had been accepted by Trinity College, Dublin, for the following September – again someone else's choice: his housemaster had said, Why not Trinity? and he agreed and sent off the forms, and they took him – and he would have been quite happy to stay at home until September came around. But everyone said, No, you must travel. What a waste of opportunity if you don't travel. So he said he would travel, and that left only the question of where he was to go.

Which is where his father came in. One of his father's friends, it appeared, had a school in Heidelberg. Why didn't he go there? Heidelberg was a beautiful city, and he could enrol in the school, and learn German.

So he had gone.

He had enrolled at the Lyceum Palatinum Heidelberg, a gracious, balconied building, overlooking the Neckar and the Old Bridge, opposite the castle.

But then the plan had broken down.

He started to learn German. He sat in class with about thirty other people. Greeks. French. Danes. Most of whom, it transpired, were freemasons. And for a while he had worked quite hard at it. But he couldn't keep it up somehow.

He hadn't really warmed to any of his fellow students. Most of them spent most of their time drinking, as far as he could see, and singing songs. One of them, a spectacularly handsome Dane called Bjorn, used to get thrown out of bars for declaiming in enormous tones some of Mussolini's less restrained speeches. Popolo Abissinio. Popolo barbaro, incivile.

He had taken to his bed. He lay there listening to everyone else getting up and going jollily down to breakfast and the morning lesson.

Then he read one or other of his books. Wherever he went he bought books. He had arrived at Heidelberg with two, and was leaving with nearly two cases. He bought them at the second hand stalls round the Heiliger Geist Kirche.

Then Herr Köchlin, his father's friend, would come in and start saying, Warum? warum? and Dies' ist kein Hotel. And he would get up. He would take his book up on to the Philosophenweg, where Goethe and Schiller used to commune with nature and each other, and spend the afternoon there, looking down over the town, and thinking, I am in Germany.

In the evening, when the rest went off to get drunk and play the Stiefel game, which involved passing round a huge beer-filled glass boot, and guzzling as much as possible, the person who didn't finish, that is to say the person before the one who did, having to pay for the boot, he walked round the town, until it was time to go back to his room and sleep.

He had to share his room. In all the time he was there he had not exchanged a single word with his roommate, and not many with anyone else.

Only one person had called him J J since he had left England. Everyone at the Lyceum, when they called him anything, called him Yustin.

I don't really know, he said. I suppose it just happened.

How nice to be so footloose, the woman said. I envy you. Now I am here for a reason.

She drank and put down her cup. He drank too, and coughed over his cigarette.

I cannot sleep, she said. You are lucky to be young, and not know the sorrow of insomnia. So I walk. And drop into places like this. My name is Magda.

Hello, Magda, he said. I was at school in Heidelberg. Learning German. I didn't learn much. I'm on way back to England. I missed the train.

And what, she said, have you learned from that?

Learned? he said.

What was there to learn?

Let us see, she said. We could start with your telling me why you are going home so obviously in the middle of term.

It was a well-known fact, his books told him, that one could say to stranger what one cannot say to anyone closer. Not that he had anyone particularly close.

Of course, and as usual, he didn't really know why, exactly why, he was leaving, why he had had enough, except that he was not the sort of person who could cope with that sort of thing. In fact, he was still waiting to discover something he could cope with, but there you are. But he could give a pretty clear outline of the last straw.

So he did.

She had asked him after all, and didn't he always do what

he was asked?

He told her. He told her about the sort of person he was, and how he spent his time at the Lyceum.

And he told her about Konradin.

Konradin was the name of a boy who had arrived about a month after he had, during the time when he still went to lessons, when he was only not enjoying it a little.

He was not – in case she had any trouble working it out – the sort of person who made friends easily. All his way through school, for instance, he had had only two. He preferred it that way. Not that he didn't envy people who found it easy to make friends. He just wasn't that sort of person.

His first two terms at school he had known no one. Then, at the beginning of his third term, there was a boy in the dormitory who asked him the way to the lavatory, and they were friends for two years.

He couldn't remember how they had quarrelled. It had something to do with a box of After Eight, his or his friend's, which either he or his friend had eaten, without reference to the other. They never spoke to each other again.

It took his next friend a year to break through to him. After a while, he found, you got used to being alone. You liked it. But he did break through. At the end of term they had gone on a long walk together, and he had gone back the next term thinking, I must not expect him to speak to me. I must not trade on one walk's worth of acquaintance.

But he did talk. And they were friends for the two years till they left. They spent every available minute together. They never parted without naming the time and place of their next meeting. I have to pee. See you back here in five minutes.

His friend was in Barcelona now, learning Spanish.

He badly missed him.

Actually, to be honest, he badly missed the life they had led together. Which was not quite the same thing.

And Konradin?

Konradin was to be his next special friend.

It was Konradin whom he wanted for his next special friend.

They had sat at the same table in the dining room, the day of Konradin's arrival. He had been very quiet. He had spent the evening playing the piano rather than out drinking.

And that was it.

That was all.

He had decided. Then, on that first evening.

Over the next few weeks, Konradin settled in to the school. He became lively at table. He did not play the piano again. He went out in the evenings and came home only slightly less drunk than the rest. But by then it was too late.

He had not said a word. He had not known how to start. He watched Konradin. At class. At meals. Whenever he could. It was good to know that he was around.

But then he stopped going to class, and didn't go to many meals, so he saw less of him.

He didn't make friends easily.

In the end, Konradin spoke to him.

It had been a tiresome day. After lunch, Herr Köchlin had obviously decided that it was time he did something for the son of his old friend, and instead of waruming and dies'-ist-kein-Hoteling, had invited him to his room for a glass of sherry.

Sherry.

After lunch.

They had a long talk. At least, Herr Köchlin spoke for a long time. There had been much hand-clasping, and What's-the-mattering, and Really, my dear Yustin, you must let me help you.

He stonewalled. He sat and looked at his feet.

Eventually Herr Köchlin gave up, and he had promised that he would try and do better. In pursuit of that promise he had gone to the afternoon lesson, on the Perfect Tense of Separable Verbs, and how to express Absence of Obligation. And he went to the evening meal where, for the first time, Konradin sat next to him, and he stared hard at his plate.

He stopped talking and drank some coffee.

He asked Magda for a cigarette.

What would life be like, she said, without coffee and cigarettes? People would never speak to each other. Neither strangers nor old friends. I'll get some more.

While she was at the counter he wiped his hands on his trousers.

More people had come into the café. Shabby people mostly. Magda looked even more out of place than ever. She came back with two more coffees and two glasses of brandy.

Like your fellow students, she said, we are going to drink. They have no Stiefel here, I'm afraid.

Oh well, he said. I couldn't afford to pay for it anyway.

You imply, she said, that I could drink the more. That is impolite. So it is, too, to emphasise that I am paying.

I'm sorry, he said.

You must learn, she said. Other people exist independently of you. They need and they feel. They have life.

I am sorry, he said.

You are sorry, she said. Where does that get us?

He stared at his hands in his lap.

We must not quarrel, she said. The night is only half over.

She lifted her glass.

Drink, she said.

They drank.

You stared at your plate, she said.

He often did. He could write a book. Plates I have known.

He had said nothing throughout the meal. Konradin was

quiet too. When the plates had been taken away, and they were waiting for Herr Köchlin to ring the bell and dismiss them, he spoke.

Are you bored, Konradin said.

He thought, What? Yes. Um. Oh God, what am I going to say? Yes, he said.

I too, Konradin said. I am very bored. The people here, they are children.

Yes, he said.

I am Konradin, Konradin said.

I know, he said.

You are Yustin, Konradin said.

J J, he said.

J J, Konradin said. He got the Js right.

Herr Köchlin rang his bell, and he was about to stand up, like everyone else. But Konradin put his hand on his arm.

Wait, he said. We were talking.

Herr Köchlin nodded at him on his way out.

I'm not really bored, he said. I just said that. I don't know what's wrong with me. I'm lonely, I think.

I'm not surprised, Konradin said. Who would not be lonely in a place like this?

The dining room was empty now, apart from them. Konradin looked out of the window at the Neckar and the illuminated castle opposite.

A beautiful view, he said. But man does not live by views alone. What are we going to do tonight? While the children drink.

I don't know, he said.

Positive thought, Konradin said. And positive action. Don't tell me you've been in Heidelberg all this time, and you can't think of anything to do. No concerts? No poetry readings. My dear J J, you have been wasting your time.

Yes, he said. I expect I have. I'm not very good on my own.

Well, Konradin said. Now you have me. And I have not been wasting my time. Tonight we will go out, and I will shew you Heidelberg. We may even get a little drunk. Like the children. But we will do it properly. I will shew you how.

So they went out.

And they got drunk.

They went to a jazz bar in the new city which was full of American soldiers who bought them beer. They moved on to a wine bar in the Hauptstrasse which was full of university students who bought them wine. They ended up playing the Stiefel game in a dirty bar in a back street by the river with a group of motor mechanics.

At eleven o'clock the landlord threw everyone out except for them and a few favoured customers, whom he gathered round a central table. He served them all a glass of schnapps, and lifted his hand for silence. Then he went to a box on the wall which had the words Spezialität Gulaschsuppe written on it in Gothic script and, with an elaborate gesture, opened it.

Inside was a picture of Hitler in the robes and armour of a Ritter. Everyone stood up and shouted Sieg Heil!

He wasn't drunk enough not to be embarrassed.

But Konradin's arm was up, and he was shouting Sieg Heil like all the rest, and soon so was he.

Then they all shouted Hoch! and downed their schnapps, and Konradin took him out.

They sat on a bench by the river after that, and he was sick. Konradin put his arm round his shoulder while he puked and gave him his handkerchief to wipe his mouth.

Now, he said, to the real business of the evening. You have had too much fresh air. What you need is a smoky room and a coffee. I know just the place.

I ought to go to bed, he said.

That too, Konradin said.

I'm not used to this, he said.

You are doing very well, Konradin said. It all comes with practice. Soon it will be second nature.

He put Konradin's handkerchief in his pocket.

He couldn't walk straight for very far, so Konradin put his arm round his waist.

The wind was cold.

They sang.

After a long while they wobbled up to a neon-lit doorway, and Konradin rang the bell.

Inside was a dim room with alcoves, into one of which they fell, and a crooning jukebox.

He heard Konradin say, Coffee for my friend and Brandy for me, and he fell asleep.

He was still drunk when he woke up.

His tie was loose.

His belt was undone.

His head was in a girl's lap.

He sat up.

His coffee was cold.

The girl was not very pretty.

Konradin was dancing with a woman who didn't look very young.

He waved at Konradin, who brought his partner back to the table.

How do you like the girls? he said. I'm afraid they don't speak English. Shall you mind?

The song on the jukebox stopped. His girl leaped to her feet and yelled, Musik! Musik! Konradin's girl jumped up and down.

They want another record, Konradin said. I don't have any money. Do you?

He scooped a handful of change on to the table and Konradin's girl disappeared with it. The music started again.

His girl put her hand on his thigh.

A waiter appeared with a tray of drinks. Konradin said, Bring the bottle.

He handed a note to the waiter, who took it and returned with a half-empty bottle of brandy.

They danced.

And drank.

And danced.

And drank again.

He paid.

When the bar closed, the girls took them back to their place.

To be honest, the thought that, whatever he was going to do, Konradin was going to be doing it in the room next door, added rather a lot to his excitement.

The only trouble was, when they got to the girls' apartment it immediately became apparent that there was no room next door.

It was a big room but there was only one of them.

And there was only one bed in it.

Konradin's girl started to undress him as soon as they arrived, and he stood very still as his girl started on him. When they were both naked he looked across at Konradin.

Konradin's body was slim and pale, and his girl clucked appreciatively at it as she took off her own clothes. She went to the bed and drew Konradin down on top of her, where he lay, kissing her and pumping her belly with his hips.

His girl took off her clothes and led him to her side of the bed. She sat on the bed and took his cock in her mouth.

It didn't do any good.

He was staring at Konradin, at Konradin's luminous body.

His girl released his cock and lay down. She must have noticed where he was looking, because she leaned across and stroked Konradin's buttocks, and smiled.

He stood by the bed.

His girl opened her arms, and her legs, and he clambered between them. They kissed for a while. She sucked his tongue down her throat, and ground her hips against his.

It didn't do any good.

It hurt his tongue. That was all he felt. An ache at the root of his tongue.

Konradin and his girl had changed position. She was concentrating on his lower half, and he was lying back against the pillow with his eyes closed.

Again his girl must have seen where he was looking, because she said something in German, and Konradin opened his eyes and looked at him. He pulled himself up the bed a little. His girl must have taken this for a signal of some sort, because she lifted her head, but Konradin pushed it back again, and said something that he couldn't hear.

His girl pushed him towards Konradin. He thought, he really did, that Konradin was going to say something. He had no idea what. Encouragement maybe. Advice maybe. But he kissed him.

His girl turned round and burrowed between his legs. Again she took his cock in her mouth.

Out of the corner of his eye, as Konradin kissed him, he could see her legs wedged up against the wall.

He pulled his mouth from Konradin's mouth, and his cock from her mouth, and climbed off the bed.

It took him forever to find his clothes. He dressed with his back to the bed. When he turned round his girl was straddling Konradin's face.

Konradin's girl was sitting on the edge of the bed. As he looked she lifted and separated Konradin's legs, licked her finger, and slid it into his anus.

She was looking at him. Her face was perfectly matter of fact.

She took her finger out of Konradin's anus and beckoned him with it.

He simply could not help himself. He followed her finger. He knelt fully clothed on the bed. She took his head in her hands, and pushed his face between Konradin's legs. It must, he thought, be tiring to keep your legs in the air for so long.

Then she took Konradin's cock and pushed it into his mouth. Konradin swung his legs over his back and crossed them, so that he was trapped.

He fought, but between them they held him there.

He couldn't breathe. He was the only one who couldn't. The others were snorting like horses. He didn't know whether they were panting with laughter or pleasure. He was in no position to find out. But in one case at least he suspected laughter.

He stopped fighting and relaxed, which may have taken the fun out of things, because Konradin's girl pulled him off Konradin, and pushed him off the bed.

Like an angry schoolteacher she took him by the ear and led him to the door.

Stark naked she led him down the stairs and into the street.

She patted his cheek, kissed him, and closed the door on him.

He got hopelessly lost on the way home. He wandered for what felt like hours. He hid whenever he chanced on some fellow wanderer.

He thought that he might never stop blushing.

It was that final kiss that did it. All the rest he could handle. More or less.

Most of his walk he spent with a raging erection.

But that pat on the face, that kiss on the forehead, they were too much.

Oh, he'd read books. He knew, at second-hand admittedly,

but he knew, about numerous situations none too different from the one he had just found himself in. He had, in fact, imagined things not too dissimilar, although his own performance had been more professional in imagination than in fact.

He knew, too, that desire often outstrips performance, or comes too late to be of any use.

And he admitted the desire. His erection bespoke it.

He could, he swore, handle that.

It was the kiss that did it.

To be dismissed in that kindly, almost motherly way. That was more than he could take. That was what made his face blaze, and sent him scuttling into corners every time he heard a step on the street.

It would take him some time to stop remembering that.

He sat down in one of the corners he had scuttled into, and hugged his knees.

He woke to grey dawn.

Six thirty by his watch.

He was lost, but after a shortish walk he came to a tramline which he followed to a stop.

He had an enormous headache.

When the tram arrived he discovered that he had lost his wallet, so he couldn't get on. His traveller's cheques were in his wallet. All of them. Silly, of course, to carry them about like that, but it was one of his neuroses. Like with his suitcases. He liked to have important things to hand. To know where they were.

He walked along the tramlines till he got his bearings.

He crossed the Old Bridge at a quarter past eight, and arrived at the Lyceum when everyone was clattering jollily down to breakfast. He met his roommate at the door of his room, but said nothing.

He spent the morning lying on his bed, trying to sleep. It came to him suddenly as he lay there that he was going home.

Today.

Tonight.

He went through his drawers looking for money. But all he could find was a five pound note and a couple of half crowns.

That stumped him for a while.

From downstairs came the sound of lessons ending, and students trooping jollily into lunch.

He waited till everything was quiet, and went down the corridor to Konradin's room. The room was empty, the sheets on both beds tumbled, so Konradin must have got back sometime.

He found a hundred and fifty marks in a drawer and took it. He figured Konradin owed him. He left his two half crowns in their place.

It didn't take him long to pack. There was not enough room for all his books and dirty clothes in his suitcase, so he went back to Konradin's room and took one of his.

When he had finished he hid the cases under his bed, and went to the bathroom to wash and shave.

Then he lay down again.

He saw Konradin again at dinner. He sat at the other end of the table and was too busy chatting and laughing to do more than wave.

He felt pretty spry considering.

He ate quickly, and did not wait for Herr Köchlin to ring his dismissal bell. People looked surprised when he got up to leave, but he had a train to catch.

He nodded to Konradin on his way out.

He felt good on the way to the station. His bags were heavy but his heart was light. But it didn't last.

There was a queue at the ticket office.

He managed to book almost the last seat on the Ostend express.

The ticket cost ninety-eight marks which left little enough to get home on.

And he missed the train.

Magda fetched more coffee and brandy.

Of course, you know your problem, she said when she got back. You realise that you haven't even once described your friend to me. All I know of him is that he is slim and pale when naked, and that could be said of many people.

Yes, he said. I know. I'm self-absorbed. It's my fault.

Other people exist, she said. You do not like it, but it is so.

She banged her coffee spoon on the table. People looked across at them. He looked at his lap.

It is so, she said.

I shall try to remember, he said.

Remember! she said. You remember too much. You have altogether too good a memory. Which is why you only had your erection looking backwards.

He could think of nothing to say.

Of course, you know, she said, what follows from everything you've been saying.

What? he said.

That all fortune is good fortune, she said.

That was too much.

He gulped.

As if it weren't all bad enough without that.

There he was, all in all, he felt justified in thinking, in a fairly lousy state, and all she could come up with was that. Some tin-pot apophthegm that solved nothing. That left everything exactly as it was.

He couldn't think why he had told her anything if she was going to miss the point like that.

He groped in his pocket for his handkerchief, because he was going to cry. When he pulled it out he saw that it was Konradin's handkerchief, still stained with his vomit.

That did it.

He cried.

Magda waited for him to stop.

While he was stopping she said something he didn't catch.

Oh well, he said. I suppose it will come right in the end.

He put the handkerchief away. Magda looked at him. She was obviously waiting for him to say something.

I shall try to see things, he said, in this new light.

She got up and went to the counter again. While she was away he realised what it was she had said.

He squirmed in his chair. He spilled his coffee. He grabbed his brandy and downed it in one, which made him choke.

The trouble was, he wasn't sure.

She had either offered him a bed for the night, or offered to share her bed with him.

That, he felt, was a point it would be as well to be clear on.

Magda came back to the table.

You'll need this, she said. They close soon. I must be going.

All she was carrying was one glass of brandy.

He looked at the brandy.

He looked at his cases.

He looked at his watch.

Yes, Magda said. You have a problem. Don't you?

They cleaned him out.

That last brandy had been a mistake.

He had gone, after Magda left, back to the station – zum Bahnhof zurück, or was it zur? He still had trouble with gender – and sat, suitcases gripped firmly in either hand, on a bench, where his eyes unfocussed, his head lolled forward on his breast, and he surrendered, reluctantly but the brandy was too much for him, to unconsciousness.

While he slept they cleaned him out.

Gently they unclasped his hands from his cases. Gently they laid him flat on the bench and rifled his pockets.

He woke to the sight of the station roof.

He didn't know where he was.

He looked at his wrist and wondered why he wasn't wearing his watch.

His neck was stiff. His mouth was dry.

Christ!

Jesus!

Jesus Christ!

He jumped to his feet. His head swam but he didn't have time to care.

Oh God! Oh God! Oh God!

His cases, his watch, his passport, his ticket, his five pound note, his marks, even *The Unquiet Grave*, all were gone. Even Konradin's handkerchief.

He turned and ran. He turned and ran back.

He sat on the bench.

He closed his eyes, but this made him feel sick, so he opened them again.

He clasped his head in his hands, but this made it swim worse than ever, so he stopped.

He felt a sudden blow to his shoulder, but when he turned there was no one there.

He retreated into his duffel coat. He turned up the hood and pulled it down over his eyes. He hunched his elbows in at the waist and thrust his hands into his pockets.

He waited.

There was something in his pocket.

This, he thought, is happening to me.

In his pocket were a ten pfennig coin and a penny.

He rubbed them together.

The station was cold. In default of anything else to do, he might as well go for a walk.

He walked off the concourse and out along a platform to where the light ended and the night hung like a curtain.

He walked up the line.

Taking care to keep his feet on the sleepers he walked and walked up the line.

The sleepers were narrowly spaced and made him take shorter strides than usual, which occupied his mind so that it was some time before he looked up to see where he was going, and was immediately arrested by the beauty of the rails.

They swept.

They curved.

They shone in the blue night.

He looked back along them to the station.

He looked forward along them into the air.

He took the two coins out of his pocket and rubbed them together again. Then he threw them as far as he could along the rails, so far that, although he listened very hard, he couldn't hear them land.

He filled his lungs with air and slowly expelled it.

He turned and started to walk back to the station.

Which is when it happened.

A line of ice ran up his spine and punched him in the neck. A line of fire ran through his limbs and a great light slapped him behind the eyes.

He ran.

He whooped.

He leaped.

He punched the air.

He ran back along the lines to the station. He ran across

the concourse and out on to the street. He ran past Magda's café. Laughing and shouting he ran until he couldn't run any more. Giggling he leaned against a wall. His legs buckled and he curled up into his duffel coat and, smiling, slept.

It was full day when he woke.

The pavement under his feet was orange.

Feet walked past his face.

A coin fell by his nose.

Rubbing his eyes he pulled himself up on to his elbow.

Around him on the pavement were chalked a parquet of lively-coloured scenes. Landscapes, Rhinescapes, portraits, a copy of Dürer's Praying Hands.

And on the pictures lay a scatter of coins.

And past him as he lay on the pictures walked Mannheim on its way to work, dropping coins and more coins around him.

He stood up, shook himself, stretched, and set about collecting the coins.

Mrs Gotts

It was this feeling. She woke up and there it was, this feeling.

She woke up into what would have been, had she examined them, a bare curtainless room with balding lino on the fourteenth floor of a tower block in Willesden, and an enormous smell of sock. But she was tired, Baby Danny had cried much of the night, indeed he was crying now, so she did not examine them. They were just the room and the smell she woke up in. She simply pulled herself out from under Jase – Jase who hadn't been there when she fell asleep for the last time, four thirty or so in the morning when Baby Danny finally settled, and who now lay snoring across her – and went to Baby Danny's room to pick him up and quiet him.

It was this feeling. She couldn't put a name to it. She wasn't the sort of person, as witness the room and the smell, to put names to things. Who has time anyway to put names to things? You just got up and got on with it. It was just this strange feeling. Under everything she did. This feeling. She hunched into slippers and house coat and went to Baby Danny's room to pick him up and quiet him.

Baby Danny's room was another bare curtainless room with balding lino, smaller though than her room and Jase's, at the end of the corridor by the bathroom. Its only furniture was a tiny hearthrug, a rucked rag rug with a pattern of ducks, and Baby Danny's cot itself, an ancient wooden structure found in the market and bought eight years ago for Baby Billy, a castered, slatted structure painted baby blue and transferred with multicoloured teddy bears, the blue and the bears picked and worn now back to the wood. Baby Billy, just plain Billy now, was still asleep, she supposed, despite Baby Danny's noise, in the room he shared with his sister. They were going to be late for school. She picked up Baby Danny, cradled him in her arms and soothed him. He had a tooth coming and was not easy to soothe. When he quietened she slung him on her hip and went to wake his brother and sister.

All with this feeling.

She woke the kids. Billy was difficult to wake. He lay sunk in sleep, his face in the pillows, and struck out at anyone who tried to wake him. Aroused, he hauled himself into sluggish motion, dressing with his eyes closed. Libby, two years his junior, woke more easily, but woke into drama. Her cherished cat, Clotilde, a shaggy piebald who shared her bed and who had been ill for several days, dripping, sulking and sniffling, had at some stage during the night vomited a saffron stripe across the pillow, and Libby had slept in it. She too had to be soothed and quietened, and Billy chivvied and hurried, to say nothing of Baby Danny, roused again by the drama, re-pacified and handed over to his sister who was more concerned with her cat, and all of this quietly, quietly or you'll wake your father, before their mother could snatch a moment or two in the bathroom and get dressed.

The feeling was still there in the bathroom. She washed and dressed. She ran a flannel, that is to say, across her face, ran a comb through her hair, and climbed into bra and panties, leggings and T-shirt. Had she looked in the mirror, no doubt she would have been surprised at what she saw. The last time she had looked, after all, she had seen a fresh and pretty girl, a girl with curled blonde hair and a smile, and now there was a slack-faced woman there, a woman with mottled skin, lank hanks where the curls had been, puffed eyes where the smile had been. But she did not look. Why would she look? All she would see was her. Just as if she had looked at her home she would have seen a succession of bare curtainless rooms with balding lino, dotted here and there with randomly acquired pieces of market furniture, and smart electrical appliances she had long since stopped asking herself, let alone Jase, where they came from. But she did not look. Why would she look? It was just where she lived.

And the feeling. Maybe she would have looked at it. Maybe she would have sat for a while and thought about it. Maybe she would. It was a strange feeling. But Baby Danny started up again, and Libby yelled from the kitchen, and if she didn't get back there sharpish Jase would wake up and then where would she be? The feeling, still there, still there, went unexamined.

And it didn't go away. Examined or not it stayed with her. All through the morning, and it was not a good morning, it was, in the end, one of those mornings, it was there.

She gave the children their breakfast, toast and jam, tea and a packet of crisps, and it was there. Baby Danny squalling on her hip, she shepherded Billy and Libby to the lift, Libby still carrying the limp Clotilde, who was to be dropped off at the PDSA after the children had been dropped off at school, and it was there. The lift was out of order, she led the children down fourteen flights of stairs, and it was there. She turned it into a sort of game. Every now and again during the course of the journey – Billy and Libby, say, whining and squabbling all the way down the stairs and into the car; Baby Danny crying on the front seat all the way to school, Billy and Libby lapsed into silence now, each staring firmly out of an opposite window; Clotilde, roused from her sickness to struggle and spit in Libby's arms when they arrived at school, lashing out and scratching Libby all down one cheek; herself, eager to get them off, impatient to get back and re-climb fourteen flights of stairs to prepare Jase's breakfast before he woke and asked for it, herself slamming the car door a fraction of a second too early and catching the tip of Billy's finger in it, and all of them having to scramble back into the car and race to the hospital, Billy shrieking with the pain, and Libby and Baby Danny shrieking in sympathy, to have the finger seen to – every now and again she took a quick dip beneath the course of things to see if it was still there. The feeling.

It was still there.

It was still there at the hospital, where she got into such a flap, what with Billy still yelling with the pain, and Libby still shrieking and refusing point blank to be left in the car, that she left Baby Danny and Clotilde by themselves on the back seat and quite frankly forgot about them till an angry nurse reminded her. It was still there at school, where she arrived in the mid-morning to find the headteacher waiting for her to say that he had had enough, that this morning's lateness was one lateness too many, that Libby was a bully, that there wasn't a girl in her class who wasn't afraid of her, that Billy was a thief, that there wasn't a thing that wasn't nailed down that was safe from him, and that he wanted to see her and Mr Gotts – and Mr Gotts now mind – as soon as possible to talk about it. It was still there in the car on the way home, with her driving much too fast in order to be home for Jase and his breakfast, Clotilde still unseen by the PDSA, she would have to go this afternoon or God knows what Libby would say. It was still there when the policeman stopped her. It was still there on the roundabout, where she realised what it was.

Halfway round the roundabout and she realised what it was. The feeling. The feeling. And the realisation startled her so much that she let go the steering wheel, and the car swerved and bucketed across one lane of traffic, then another, and on to the central island before she regained control of it. But it didn't matter because, as she drove off the island back on to the road, it was still there, the feeling, and she didn't care. She didn't care about anything, and she took the roundabout once, twice, three times more out of sheer happiness.

Who Loves You?

My mother sent the cheque to my office. I read it and folded it into my wallet. I looked through her letter, tore it and the envelope in half, and put the pieces in the wastepaper basket. There was shred of bacon wedged between two of my back teeth. I sucked, and probed at it with my fingers, but I couldn't dislodge it. I finally worried it out with a straightened paper clip.

Before starting work I looked into my wallet and the wastepaper basket to make sure I hadn't torn up the cheque by mistake. I took the cheque out and looked at it several times during the morning. I had never seen a cheque for so much before.

At lunchtime I took the cheque to my bank and deposited it. I folded the receipt into my wallet. Just after I got back it came on to rain. It rained heavily till about three o'clock. I took the receipt out and looked at it several times during the afternoon.

I was late home. The buses were difficult. I hate it when I can't get a seat. On the way home from the bus stop I patted my wallet through my jacket several times. As I came down the area steps I could see Stevie playing his guitar. I stood at the door with my key in my hand and listened. Stevie likes to play the guitar.

I went straight through to the kitchen and started to prepare a salad. I put my briefcase down by the fridge. I washed a lettuce, and sliced tomatoes and made a vinaigrette dressing. I could still hear the sound of Stevie's guitar from the sitting room. Stevie wants to be a professional singer. He writes his own songs, and sings them into the tape recorder. I put the kettle on for coffee, and tripped over my briefcase. I kicked it into a corner, ground some coffee beans, and waited for the kettle to boil.

While the coffee was filtering I went to the bathroom. The window was open and there was a puddle of rain on the floor. I mopped up the water, finished making my coffee, and took the cup through into the bedroom. I would have lain down, but I noticed there were no pillows on the bed. Not only were there no pillows on the bed but there were no cushions on any of the chairs.

I went back to the bathroom and ran a bath. I picked up my briefcase from where I'd kicked it, and sorted my papers for the morning. I laid out tomorrow's clothes, hung up today's, finished my coffee, and had a shave and a bath. It came on to rain again when I was in the bath, and rain came in the window. I got out of the bath to close the window, and made more mess than if I'd just let the rain come in.

There were still no pillows on the bed when I got back to the bedroom. I couldn't hear Stevie's guitar any more, so I went into the sitting room. Stevie was sitting on a mountain of pillows and cushions in the middle of the floor. He'd taken every cushion and pillow in the place and made a pile of them. He was hugging his guitar and staring out of the window. We live in a basement. He jumped up when I came in, and swallowed. Stevie has enormous eyes.

Stevie, I said. I'm going to lie down.

I took the pillows from the pile.

I'll lay the table, shall I? he said.

Please, I said. I need to lie down for a while.

Stevie started putting the cushions back, and I went to lie down. I closed my eyes, and Stevie came in with the bedroom cushions. I could hear him moving quietly round the room, leaving cushions here and there. I kept my eyes closed. When I thought he'd gone I opened my eyes, and he was standing in the door looking at me. He smiled. Stevie has a shy smile.

I dozed for half an hour. Then I got up and went to the kitchen to cook. I grilled some steaks. Stevie had laid the table. We had steak and a salad, and biscuits and cheese. While we ate Stevie played his tapes.

After supper Stevie washed up and made coffee, and we sat on the sofa to watch television. We watched two comedies and the news. Then Stevie had a bath and I did some work. There was a shred of steak wedged between two of my back teeth. I couldn't dislodge it. I finally picked it out with a broken match. At half past ten Stevie brought me a cup of tea. He was wearing my dressing gown, a striped kimono that I belt with an old silk scarf. He'd wrapped the scarf twice round his waist and knotted it. It only goes once round mine. Stevie is as tall as I am.

I sat on the sofa and drank my tea. I lay back, and Stevie massaged my forehead, my temples and my shoulders. We went to bed, and Stevie sucked my dick for a while, and beat off. It takes Stevie a long time to beat off.

After he'd finished we leaned back against the pillows and smoked a cigarette. I turned out the light.

We ought to talk, Stevie said.

I don't know what you want, he said. You haven't told me.

Right now, I said, I want to sleep. We can talk some other time. We never talk.

What are we going to do? he said.

I'm going to buy this place, I said. My own flat. The money came through today. For the deposit. What are you going to do?

He didn't answer. We went to sleep.

It was after midnight when I woke up. I like to get eight hours sleep. I can't work properly if I'm tired. It makes me feel ill. I was alone in the bed. The bathroom light was on. I turned on the bedroom light and smoked a cigarette. I took out the receipt and looked at it. I went to the bathroom. The door bumped against Stevie as I opened it. He was kneeling on the floor in front of the sink, bent over, with his head on his arms.

Stevie, I said. For God's sake. What are you doing? Come back to bed.

He turned and looked at me. Stevie has enormous eyes. I looked away. He got up and followed me into the bedroom. In bed he held me very tight and I kissed him. He sat on me and I fucked him. Stevie is very beautiful. I wanted to hit him. I wanted to love him. Afterwards he held me, and I wanted to sleep, but he wouldn't leave me alone. He stroked me and pushed me and pulled me. I didn't react. I waited for him to stop. He lifted my arm and dropped it on to his chest.

I love it when you're like this he said. I can do anything with you.

He picked up my arm and dropped it again. He pulled my face towards him and kissed me.

Stevie, I said. I must sleep.

I curled up on my side. I was careful not to look at the clock. The bathroom light was still on, and when I went to turn it off I noticed that the cap of my aftershave was off. It must have been off since my shave. It was expensive aftershave. I put the cap back on and went back to bed. Stevie had turned off the light. I lay awake for a long time. I didn't move. I was going to feel dreadful tomorrow. I felt Stevie sit up and lean over me. He kissed my cheek. I didn't move. He must have thought I was asleep, because he started talking.

God, he said. Over and over. God. Please God. Help us.

Us, I thought.

Big Ears and the Star Man

There he is on the canal.

It's eight o'clock on a summer evening. A late summer evening. August, September, maybe. September, because he's back at school. It's eight o'clock on a September evening, a hot evening glooming over to rain, and he's walking home along the canal.

Big Ears.

He's walking slowly. He's tired. He's been to the track. He's spent his usual after-school three hours at the track. His legs are stiff. His arms ache. His ears are ringing and he has a split lip. His right eye is swollen, closing, throbbing. Tomorrow it will be black. He's walking slowly home along the canal. He walks slowly out from under the bridge, slowly past the keeper's hut, slowly along the hedge, and he sees him, out on his balcony.

The Star Man.

Big Ears on the canal. The Star Man out on his balcony.

Time was he would have been home by now. Big Ears. Home for hours by now. Time was he would have hung around the playground hugging his book-bag, head hooked in the hood of his parka, till everyone was gone. It didn't take long for everyone to go, and he would skulk home along the canal, dragging his feet, running his ruler along the railings, making noise for company. Time was he didn't go to the track. Didn't even think of the possibility of going to the track. Didn't even know the track was there, along the canal, just a mile or so further along the canal.

Time Was was before Mr Digby.

The Star Man lives by the canal. The Star Man lives in a long low flat, the last of a series, on the other side of the canal. His flat is on the ground floor. It has, like all the flats in the block – a long, low block, two storeys high, the second storey set back from the first, the roof of the first forming a terrace for the second – a long low balcony, separated from the towpath on the other side of the canal by a long low wall.

The Star Man was Mr Digby's friend.

Up till now, Time Was had been before Mr Digby.

Now, Big Ears thinks, there are two sorts of Time Was. There is, he thinks, turning sharply to the left after the keepers's hut, and ducking out of the gate, there is Time Was, the way you used to be. And there is Time Was, yesterday. This, Big Ears thinks, creeping behind the bushes that run along the canal fence, and crouching down to watch the Star Man's balcony through a gap in the branches, this, the way time, no matter how long and various, had always seemed to separate only into two, into Now and Not Now, but now had suddenly subdivided, this is something he should think about, is something arresting, is something which, time was, he would have asked Mr Digby about.

For example, Time Was, the way things used to be, a snapshot:

We are in the boys' toilets, high in Block C. The floor is awash with liquid, the walls ascrawl with tags and graffiti. The drain to the urinal, a scarred steel trough running loosely down the north wall, is blocked with wadded paper, and each flush sends a further wave of water and sodden cigarette ends out across the floor. In the cubicles the pedestals are also blocked, their stained plastic seats cracked, or smashed, or simply absent. A paper-towel dispensing machine is hanging by one screw to the wall. The smell is enormous. This is not a room where anyone would voluntarily spend more time than he has to. And yet here is a boy, crouched on the bowl in a locked cubicle, hugging his knees, his feet drawn up on to the seat, struggling with indifferent success to control his breathing. He has been running. He is Big Ears.

And here is another boy. He too has been running. He has been chasing Big Ears up and down corridors and stairs, and has run him to earth here, in the C Block lavatories. He too is breathing fast and hard. He is not pleased at having been made to run, and less pleased at having to plash his way across a watery floor to catch his quarry. He kicks open door after cubicle door, shouting as he does so. He is Chris Humphries.

Right then, he shouts. Right then, little Big Ears. Right then, Big Ears. I know you're in here.

Big Ears in his cubicle holds his breath, listening to the sound of approaching feet. The feet stop at his door. There is a bang on the door. Big Ears crouches smaller on his seat.

Right then, Chris Humphries says outside the door. Come on out, Big Ears. I know you're in there.

Big Ears sits.

Chris Humphries leans on the door.

Come on out, Big Ears, he says. You know I've got you. You might as well come out.

He bangs thunderously on the door. Big Ears within begins quietly to cry.

Come on Big Ears, Chris Humphries says.

Big Ears. Big Ears.

Big Ears covers his ears.

That was Time Was. That was definitely Time Was. His ringing ears, his aching arms, his split lip and closing eye, all attest that that was Time Was, the way things used to be.

And then again, there was Time Was, yesterday:

Time was, on the way back from the track, running along the canal, back from the track, that he would not have swerved.

He would have come out from under the bridge and called. He would have run out past the keeper's hut, calling. Run down along the hedge calling and waving. And he would have stopped.

Hi, he would have said.

And the Star Man, out on his balcony, his stars out, out on his balcony, would have looked up across the canal, and smiled, and said Hi too. And they would have talked for a while.

That was why he ran home along the canal. So that the Star Man would say Hi, and they could talk for a while.

Then, admittedly, when they had talked, and when the Star Man had gone back to what he was doing before Big Ears arrived, sitting usually, out on his balcony, his shirt off and his stars out, out on his balcony, then, admittedly, Big Ears would have ducked out of the gate. He would have run on till he was out of sight, then turned and ducked through the other, the far gate, and crawled back along the hedge to look at the Star Man through the gap in the branches. But he would have done it after the talking. After the calling, the smiling, the saying Hi.

But now all that was over. That was another thing the split lip and the cut eye meant. The aching arms and the ringing ears. There would be no more calling, no more smiling, no more saying Hi and talking. There would be just this. Waiting behind the hedge. Watching the Star Man through the hedge. Waiting for Mr Digby.

There was Time Was, no matter how subdivided, and there was Now. Time was he could have spoken to Mr Digby about it.

The Star Man was Mr Digby's friend.

It was Mr Digby who got Big Ears to the track.

It was Mr Digby who, looking out of the staff room window saw Big Ears put on an extra streak of speed across the quad, with Chris Humphries, hitherto Mr Digby's fastest and fiercest, left panting behind, and race up the stairs of Block C. It was Mr Digby who followed Chris Humphries up the stairs and into the boys' lavatory, and plashed across the flooded floor to take him by the ear and eject him. Mr Digby who busied himself unblocking drains and running taps until Big Ears came out of the cubicle. Mr Digby who listened to the long outflowing of Big Ears' misery. Mr Digby who undertook to do something about it. To do, indeed, the one thing about it that would stop it, to neutralise Chris Humphries.

How he did this Big Ears never knew. Mr Digby was not a man in whom it was possible to have much confidence. In class, which was the only place Big Ears had seen him – he taught French and Italian – he could keep no order and was prone to amusing outbursts of rage for which he always apologised, during which he promised dire punishment which he always withdrew. It was well known that you could run rings round Mr Digby. But he did it. Big Ears was not troubled by Chris Humphries again. The next time Big Ears saw him he looked away. The time after that he nodded. They passed in the corridor and Chris Humphries let out a muttered, All right? By the end of the week, after Mr Digby had taken Big Ears aside and asked him to join him for his training sessions at the track, and Big Ears had, to his surprise, found himself agreeing, Chris Humphries was grinning at him. They went to the track together.

Big Ears found out where the Star Man lived as follows:

It all happened along the canal. The school was on the canal. A mile to the west Big Ears lived with his parents in a tower block on an estate on the canal. Three miles to the east the track was on the canal. Mr Digby decided that he was to run. His strength lay in running. Chris Humphries' strength, Mr Digby had already decided, lay in boxing. So, after Throwaround, after the warm up session and a couple of rounds of circuit work, Chris Humphries went to the ring and Big Ears ran. To begin with Mr Digby ran with him, but pretty soon he couldn't keep up and Big Ears ran by himself. He ran round the track. He ran round and round the track. He ran faster and longer than anyone else. And he ran home. This was his idea. At seven o'clock the session was over. At seven o'clock they all stopped what they were doing, Chris Humphries left the ring, Big Ears left the track, everyone else, ring or gym or track, stopped what they were doing, they all had a shower and they went home. It was Big Ears' idea to get back into his running kit and run the three miles home along the canal.

Every day, running home along the canal.

There he was, then, running. He ran two miles from the track, he ran past warehouse and cemetery, houseboat, bus garage and church. He ran under the mile-long sweep of the flyover. Pump those arms, he thought, as Mr Digby had told him. Think piston, he thought. Think internal combustion. He ran till he came out from under the bridge. He ran along the gardens. He was passing the keeper's hut when he saw him, the Star Man, out on his balcony, and he stopped short.

It was high summer and the Star Man was sitting on his balcony wall. His shirt was off, his stars were out, his feet were bare, and he was talking to someone. He and the someone sat facing each other, astraddle the wall. As Big Ears stopped short the someone swung his leg out over the wall and jumped off the balcony on to the path. And the Star Man swore at him.

What the fuck are you doing? the Star Man said.

The Star Man was French. What de ferk? he said.

The someone looked up, confused.

Huh? he said.

That is not fucking clever, the Star Man said. You know what is like round here. What do you think they are going to think? If they see you jumping off my balcony?

The someone was still confused.

Huh? he said again.

Easy, the Star Man said. Is what they're going to think. You can jump off, you can jump on is what they're going to think. I don't need anyone being told is easy to jump on my fucking balcony, you know?

The someone lifted soothing hands.

Ok, he said, Ok. Shit, I just jumped off the wall.

OK, the Star Man said. It's my wall, OK? I have to live here.

Big Ears watched as the someone walked off. He watched the someone out of sight. When he looked back the Star Man was looking at him across the canal.

Hi, the Star Man said.

He was sitting on the wall facing outwards now, facing Big Ears across the canal. Big Ears on the canal. The Star Man sitting on his balcony wall. The width of the canal between them.

Hi, Big Ears said.

Out running, the Star Man said.

He scratched his naked chest. Even from the other side of the canal Big Ears could see his stars. Cassiopeia on his arm, Boötes on his chest, Betelgeuse on his stomach, peeping over the waistline of his underpants, itself peeping over the waistline of his jeans. There was a plaster on his naked foot. His right foot.

Uh, yeah, Big Ears said.

The Star Man swung his feet. He crossed his legs at the ankle, swung them out and back, out and back. He looked up at the sky.

Lovely evening, he said.

Yeah, Big Ears said.

The Star Man closed his eyes.

I should go, Big Ears said.

The Star Man lifted a hand.

Sure, he said.

Big Ears didn't move.

You live here, Big Ears said.

The Star Man's eyes stayed closed.

Sure, he said.

I run here every night, Big Ears said.

The Star Man leaned back on the wall.

So, he said. That is nice. I expect we'll maybe see each other quite a bit.

Big Ears ran on. He ran on till he was out of sight. Then he turned and ducked through the far gate into the park and crawled back along the hedge to look at the Star Man through the gap in the branches. The Star Man sat on his wall, his legs crossed at the ankle, his eyes closed, his face turned to the sky. Then he swung back on to his balcony, peeled off his jeans and stood in his underpants. Then he sat down and Big Ears couldn't see him any more.

They called themselves The Losers' Club. This was Mr Digby's idea. He was very strict about it. The less they felt like losers at the track the stricter he was about it. We are losers, after all, he said. The only place we're not losers, after all, he said, is this place. And it's important to acknowledge where you come from. No matter how far you go you must always remember where you come from. So we don't care, right? We're proud of it, right? They try to put us down, he said, but do we go down?

Well, he said. Do we?

No, they said.

So we're The Losers then, he said. Are we? And how do we feel about it? he said. Do we feel bad?

No, they said.

Do we feel proud? he said.

Yes, they said.

Too right, Mr Digby said.

And they were losers, Big Ears knew. You just had to look at them. Look at Chris Humphries, smoking alone in the playground toilets, hanging round the bike sheds, mugging juniors for their lunch money. Look at him, look at Big Ears, shuffling round the playground, hugging the fence, head hooked in the hood of his parka. Look the rest of them, anoraks and ruler-tappers the lot of them. All of them, without Mr Digby, a crew of losers. And Mr Digby himself. Too right, Big Ears thought. The biggest loser of them all.

For example, Mr Digby as loser, a snapshot:

It is winter. It is last winter. It is February. Half past three on a February afternoon, a gray sky glooming over towards evening, and thick snow on the ground. Big Ears is hanging round the playground, head hooked in the hood of his parka, waiting for the playground to empty. He is standing by the fence, running his ruler along the railings. Outside the fence a few late teachers are walking towards the station, one of them Mr Digby. Big Ears watches as they walk along the fence. They are silent, their breath smokes on the cold air, their feet crunch over the snow. Suddenly, from behind the corner of the playground comes a yell and a barrage of snowballs. The teachers are engulfed in snow. They laugh. They pick up snowballs themselves and throw them back at the giggling ambush of small boys. All except Mr Digby. His snowball has hit him in the face and dislodged his glasses. He picks the snow from his face and blinks round for his glasses. He finds them in the snow. He bends to pick them up, and as he holds them up – the bridge, Big Ears sees through the fence, is broken, they will not sit on his face, to see through them Mr Digby has to hold them up to his eyes – as he holds them up another snowball hits him, this time on the chest. He runs. There is silence. Silence from the teachers. Silence from the snowballing boys. They watch in silence as Mr Digby runs, as fast as he can, away down the street, his feet slipping and skidding on the snow.

Mr Digby's glasses, by the way, have not been mended since. They are held together across the bridge with a piece of sticking plaster. The same sort of sticking plaster, Big Ears knows, that the Star Man uses on his feet.

It was only at the track that they weren't losers.

Chris Humphries in the ring, Big Ears on the track, the gym team, swinging and springing on box and bars, you couldn't call them losers. Anyone, Big Ears said, who saw Mr Digby organising teams and supervising sessions at the track, anyone who saw him sparring with Chris Humphries, running with Big Ears, swinging and springing with the gym team, who saw him catching balls, throwing balls, kicking balls at the end of the day, and saw him in French class at the beginning of the next, mumbling and shambling, losing his temper and apologising, everyone running rings round him, making him promise dire punishments and later withdraw them, they'd never have guessed it was the same man.

Why do you do it? Big Ears asked as they ran round the track – this was when they talked, circuit after circuit of the track, this was when Big Ears would have told Mr Digby about Time Was, for instance, were they still talking – why are you like this?

Why are you like it? Mr Digby said, his voice even, his breath barely rising from the run, why do you do it? Why are you like you are here, and like you are there?

I'm a loser, Big Ears said, sharpening the pace. I'm a loser, right?

You better believe it, Mr Digby said. We're all losers here, right?

And he ran off to the gym to swing and spring, to the ring to box.

Only nobody did see. Nobody came to see. Or when they did – it happened once, the Headmaster and the Deputy came, they'd heard rumours and came to see for themselves

– when they did there was nothing to see. Everything fell to bits. Mr Digby, who met them at the door with a new haircut, the messy old curls banished, replaced with a sleek crop – for fuck's sake, Chris Humphries said, what does he think he's doing? makes him look about twelve years old; makes him look, he said punching Big Ears on the shoulder, about as old as you – Mr Digby mumbled and shambled, and tripped over his laces. The gym team's pyramid fell over. The visitors stayed to watch neither Chris Humphries in the ring nor Big Ears on the track. They exchanged a glance and left after quarter of an hour.

It doesn't matter, Mr Digby said later on the track. Circuit after circuit with Big Ears on the track. Why should it matter? This is here. That is there. This is our secret, right?

Till the Star Man came.

Till, one day in early May, a day or so after Mr Digby's new haircut, at Throwaround. They began each session at the track with Throwaround, and finished with Kickaround. Kickaround was a football free for all. Throwaround meant they all stood around a cricket cradle, a slatted, hammock-shaped structure into which you threw a cricket ball, and caught it when it bounced out. The slatted, hammock shape meant that you could never tell which way it would bounce. At Throwaround suddenly there he was, standing between Big Ears and Mr Digby, jumping at every ball that flew at him, and laughing when he failed to catch it.

Which is how it started. Which is how whatever it was started that led to this: to Big Ears crouched behind the hedge on the other side of the canal, to peering through the branches at the Star Man on his balcony, to time cut in two, to Now and Not now, to a swollen eye, ringing ears and a split lip, to watching and waiting, waiting for Mr Digby.

That was the beginning of it.

He wasn't very good at the track, the Star Man. He joined

in everything. He boxed with Chris Humphries, and lost. He swang and sprang with the gym team, not very well. He ran with Big Ears, neither very fast nor very far. He wasn't very good at anything. But he always laughed when he failed so you didn't mind. Nobody minded. Nobody but Chris Humphries minded.

Chris Humphries minded badly.

I don't see why he has to be here all the time, he said. He's no good. It's not as if he was any good at anything or anything.

The only thing he was good at was Kickaround. He played in goal, and it was not often that the ball got past him. Chris Humphries had played in goal before the Star Man arrived, and quite a few balls had got past him. He didn't thank you if you pointed this out to him.

The Star Man drove a blue mini, and at the end of the session he and Mr Digby drove away in it. This annoyed Chris Humphries more than anything else. Sometimes Big Ears would find Chris Humphries staring after the departing mini and swearing.

Fuck that, he would say. Just fuck that, OK? I'm not having that.

Big Ears thought the Star Man was wonderful. Big Ears saw the Star Man and he got a lump in his chest. The Star Man appeared next to Big Ears running round the track and Big Ears ran a little faster out of sheer pleasure that the Star Man was there, until he realised that the Star Man didn't know how to run, and if he ran faster the Star Man couldn't keep up and would drop away, so he ran slower. He told the Star Man how to run. Pump those arms, he said. Think piston, he said. Think internal combustion.

Big Ears and the Star Man, a snapshot:

They are by the water cooler. Big Ears has been spotting Chris Humphries at his bench presses, and the Star Man has been working at the pec-deck. Big Ears sees the Star Man heading for the water cooler, apologises to Chris Humphries and goes for a drink. At the water cooler he talks to the Star Man.

Hi, he says.

The Star Man gasps and wipes his face.

Hard work, he says.

The Star Man is French. Ard Werrk, he says.

On the Star Man's finger, Big Ears sees, is a sticking plaster, folded round the first joint of his left index finger.

Cut your hand? he says.

The Star Man looks at his hand.

You know French? he says. You know the letters in French? he says. You know V, R, U?

Yes, Big Ears says.

So then, the Star Man says. You know what it is.

Big Ears looks at him.

C'est une verrue, the Star Man says. A wart. Not so pretty. I keep it covered up.

Another snapshot:

They are by the tea urn, Chris Humphries and Big Ears. They are taking a break. They are sitting on a bench and talking, and the Star Man comes in. His face is green. He sags on to a bench next to Big Ears and leans his head between his knees.

I feel sick, he says. Oh my God, how I feel sick.

He pants. Sweat from his forehead drops into a pool between his feet. He pants and pants. Chris Humphries looks at Big Ears and grins. The Star Man leans back against the wall.

Never, he says. Never would I have started if I knew it would be like this.

His face is green. Chris Humphries laughs. The Star Man turns to look at him. He laughs too.

Never, he says. And now I am sick, he says. I am sick and nobody cares.

Chris Humphries opens his mouth. Big Ears, sitting next to him, sitting between him and the Star Man, hears him open his mouth and guesses what he is going to say. He coughs to cover the sound.

When the Star Man has gone there are the marks of his sweat on the bench. There are marks left by his buttocks on the bench, the pool between his feet, marks left by his shoulders and head against the wall. Big Ears waits for Chris Humphries to go, then takes a handkerchief out of his pocket, soaks it in the Star Man's sweat, and folds it back into his pocket again.

A third snapshot:

The changing room. Big Ears, walking with Chris Humphries away towards the gym, has seen the Star Man arrive, and made an excuse to go back to his locker. Shit, he has said. My watch. I've still got my watch on. You go on. I won't be long. And he has gone back to the changing room to see the Star Man.

The Star Man is changing. The Star Man has taken off his shirt, and is sitting down to take off his socks. On his chest and arm Big Ears can see his stars. He knows what they are. He has stolen from the school library a pocket star atlas and has looked them up. On his left bicep is Cassiopeia. On his left breast Boötes.

I like your stars, he says.

The Star Man smiles.

I like them too, he says.

He bends down and pulls off his sock. On his foot are two pieces of sticking plaster. Big Ears points at them.

Des verrues, he says.

Certainly, the Star Man says. You never know what you are going to catch. Here in the gym. It is a sacrifice to come, yes?

Does it hurt? Big Ears says. To have them done. The stars.

It hurts a little, the Star Man says. No pain, no gain, yes?

Big Ears thought the Star Man was just wonderful.

When he found out where the Star Man lived he went there every day. Every day after track, eight o'clock in the evening, there he would be running home along the canal. Usually the Star Man was out on his balcony. Sometimes not. Usually the Star Man was alone. Sometimes not. Sometimes Mr Digby was with him. Every evening Big Ears would run out from under the bridge, run calling and waving past the keeper's hut, along the hedge, and stop opposite the Star Man's balcony to call Hi across the canal. Every evening they would chat for a while, and then Big Ears would run on till he was out of sight, turn and duck through the far gate into the park, and crawl back along the hedge to look at the Star Man through the gap in the branches.

Most evenings the Star Man just sat on his balcony. When he sat Big Ears could see little more than the top of his head. Sometimes people visited. They sat on the balcony, drinking and smoking, and chatted. Sometimes people would come and sit on the balcony and the Star Man would cut their hair. He cut Mr Digby's hair. Breathless behind the hedge, his arm aching from holding down a branch, Big Ears would sit sometimes for as long as an hour, watching the Star Man. Sometimes, greatly daring he would run a bit further on to the next bridge, cross the canal, and run back on the Star Man's side. When he got near the end of the Star Man's block he would crouch down under the long, low wall, and sit on the path directly under the Star Man's Balcony. This he did only when the Star Man was alone, and only for a few minutes at a time. His heart beat too fast for any longer. It beat so fast and so loud he was amazed the Star Man couldn't hear it from behind the wall. He was so close he could hear the Star Man breathe. The Star Man talked a lot on the phone. He talked in French.

Once, when he was sitting under the wall, the Star Man sitting quiet on the balcony, Mr Digby came suddenly out from the flat and Big Ears held his breath while they talked. They talked in French, too glib and fast for Big Ears to understand, and he could hear their breath between the words.

Mr Digby and the Star Man.

June, July, August. Big Ears on the canal. The Star Man, with or without Mr Digby, on his balcony.

It ended because of Chris Humphries:

Chris Humphries didn't like the Star Man. Chris Humphries didn't trust the Star Man further than he could throw him. Just the sight of the Star Man was enough for Chris Humphries. He saw Mr Digby and the Star Man together and he swore. He saw Mr Digby and the Star Man drive away in the Star Man's blue mini, and he wasn't having it. Fuck that, he said. Just Fuck that, OK? I'm not having that.

The end, a snapshot:

They are at Kickaround. Mr Digby and the Star Man have just left. They are walking together back to the gym to shower and change. Chris Humphries and Big Ears are staring after them, Chris Humphries, as usual, swearing.

Just you wait, he says. Just you fucking wait.

That guy is trouble, he says. Just you wait and see. Any day now and that man will be trouble.

He's a friend, Big Ears says. He's just a friend. He's Mr Digby's friend, that's all.

Chris Humphries looks at him.

Yeah right, Chris Humphries says. And we sure know what sort of friend, don't we? I don't believe you, he says. I mean, are you thick, or what? he says. We don't need friends like that around the place. You come with me, I'll show you what sort of friends they are.

He takes Big Ears by the arm and pulls him away from the game. He pulls him across the field to the gym, through the gym, past water cooler and tea urn, to the changing room door.

Friends, he says. You wait. I've seen what sort of friends they are. I've seen what they do. You wait.

He opens the changing room door. From behind the lockers comes the sound of splashing water. Chris Humphries holds his finger to his lips and pushes Big Ears into the room.

Just walk in, Chris Humphries whispers from behind his finger. We'll just get undressed and walk in, and then you'll see.

He follows Big Ears into the room, pulling off his shirt.

Come on, he says. We've got to be quick. And quiet, he says. We've got to be quiet.

Quickly then, and quietly, they get out of their clothes. Wrapped in towels they make for the showers. Steam and the sound of rushing water pour out from the shower room door.

Go on, Chris Humphries says. You go first.

He walks ahead of Chris Humphries to the door. Suddenly he feels a hand at his waist as Chris Humphries pulls away his towel, another at his back as Chris Humphries pushes him naked into the room. He hears the sound of laughter over the rushing water as Chris Humphries runs away.

It is not Mr Digby and the Star Man under the shower. It is just the Star Man. Big Ears skids in under the water and the Star Man jumps.

My God, he says. Oh it's you. You startled me.

He smiles. He is soaping himself under the stream.

Big Ears stares.

Come in then, the Star Man says.

He holds out his soap.

Come in, he says. Wash.

Big Ears takes the soap. The Star Man turns on the shower next to his and gestures Big Ears under it. Big Ears steps under the shower and for a while all he can hear is the pound of water against his skull. He closes his eyes. He does not intend to open them until the Star Man has gone, but after a while he does, and there is the Star Man smiling at him.

Good, yes? the Star Man says.

Big Ears soaps his hair. The Star Man twists and turns under his shower. Big Ears rinses his hair.

Let me, the Star Man says. You've missed a bit. Let me.

He cups his hand under the shower stream and fills it with water.

Turn round, he says.

Big Ears turns round and feels the Star Man's hand brush across the back of his head and his shoulders.

There, the Star Man says. You can turn round now.

Big Ears turns round again. Under the water the Star Man's stars gleam. Cassiopeia on his arm. Boötes on his chest. On his stomach Betelgeuse and Bellatrix, the beginning of Orion.

The Star Man sees where he is looking and himself turns round.

I have another one, he says. See?

On the Star Man's back, on his right shoulder blade, starting on his spine and spreading across the shoulder blade to his flank, is another constellation.

What is it? he says. Which one is it? Can you see?

He turns under the water and the stars gleam.

Can you see? he says.

Big Ears can see. He knows the name. He starts to say it but his voice catches and he has to start again.

It's Aquila, he says. Aquila, the eagle.

The Star Man turns again under the water.

Yes, he says. Aquila the eagle.

Big Ears clears his throat.

I know the star too, he says. The name of the star.

What star? the Star Man says. The stars have names too?

Only one, Big Ears says. Only one in Aquila.

Which one? the Star Man twists and says. Show me.

No, he says, as Big Ears points. No, I can't see. Show me.

Big Ears reaches out and touches the star on the Star Man's back.

This one, he says.

Ah, the Star Man says. And what is it called, this star?

Altair, Big Ears says.

The Star Man turns round again. They are facing each other under their showers.

Ah, the Star Man says. Altair. And the others, they have names too?

He touches Cassiopeia on his arm.

Here? he says.

No, Big Ears says. Not in Cassiopeia

Here then?

He takes Big Ears hand and runs it over the stars of Boötes on his chest. Big Ears finger stops at the largest star.

This one, he says. Arcturus.

And here? the Star Man says.

He runs Big Ears finger down his chest to his stomach, to Betelgeuse in Orion. Orion, Big Ears sees, stretches from the Star Man's stomach down past his groin to his thigh. The Star Man moves his finger from star to star.

Betelgeuse, Big Ears says, and Bellatrix.

Rigel, he says, his finger on the Star Man's thigh, and Saiph.

The Star Man didn't come to the track again.

When Big Ears left the changing room he saw Mr Digby sitting by himself at the tea urn. He was sitting with a cold cup of tea in front of him, looking down at the table, and he didn't look up as Big Ears passed. The Star Man wasn't out on his balcony when Big Ears ran out from under the bridge, but he swerved anyway, out off the path, out through the near gate, the gate by the keeper's cottage, into the park and behind the hedge, so that he wouldn't have to see him even if he was. He ran through the park and back on to the canal by the far gate. He ran, thinking pump those arms, thinking pump those arms, thinking piston, thinking internal combustion, the mile home, the mile past his home to the school. At the school he stopped, ran on the spot for a while, and turned and ran home again.

Things went on at the track without the Star Man much the same as they had before he arrived. There was Throwaround and Kickaround. There was Warm Up and Cool Down. The gym team swang and sprang. Chris Humphries trained for the ring. Big Ears ran round the track. The only change was with Mr Digby. He swang and sprang with the team. He fought with Chris Humphries. But he didn't run with Big Ears. He didn't talk and run with Big Ears. And you could see that, although he swang and sprang, it wasn't like before. When he fought, it wasn't like before. He just did it, you could see. He did it for as long as it took, and then he stopped doing it. There was no blue mini to drive him home now. Now he walked.

Only Big Ears knew where he went when he left.

He ran home, Big Ears, every night. Every night he ran out from under the bridge, not calling, not waving, and there was the Star Man, out on his balcony. Every night he swerved at the keeper's hut and ran out into the park. Every night he ducked down behind the hedge, crept along it till he was opposite the Star Man on his balcony, when he sat down and watched the Star Man through a gap in the branches. Usually the Star Man was alone. Sometimes people visited. They sat on the balcony, drinking and smoking, and chatted. Sometimes people would come and sit on the balcony and the Star Man would cut their hair. Mr Digby never came. His hair grew longer and curled again, but he never came. Breathless behind his hedge, his arm aching from holding down a branch, Big Ears would sit sometimes for as long as an hour, watching the Star Man.

Until one evening:

It is late. It is nine o'clock. Big Ears has been behind the hedge for almost an hour and is thinking of going home. The Star Man is out on his balcony. He has set up his ironing board and is doing his ironing. He is ironing sheets and jeans, shirts and towels. Big Ears can see Cassiopeia on his arm, Boötes on his chest moving as he irons. His arm is aching, aching from holding down the branch, and he is about to let it go when he hears the sound of feet along the canal. Running feet along the canal. He recognises the feet. They have run along-side him often enough for him to recognise them. He recognises too, what they are doing. He has done it often enough himself.

The feet run out from under the bridge. They swerve at the keeper's hut, and start across the grass. Big Ears just has time to drop his branch and pull further back into the hedge, back, back, back into the hedge, before he sees Mr Digby arrive. Mr Digby creeps along the hedge until he is opposite the Star Man's balcony. Then he sits down and watches the Star Man through the branches. He pulls back Big Ears' branch, and watches the Star Man through the gap. Big Ears hardly dares breathe. He sits in the hedge, watching Mr Digby through the branches as he watches through the branches, hardly daring to breathe, the Star Man across the water.

The Star Man. Cassiopeia on his arm. Boötes on his chest. Doing his ironing.

He does it every night now. He is doing it now. That's what he is doing now, sitting under the hedge, sitting deep in the hedge, watching the Star Man, watching the Star Man's stars. His right eye is swollen, closing, throbbing. Tomorrow it will be black. His ears are ringing and he has a split lip. Time is cut in two. Into Now and Not now. And he's watching in the hedge. Waiting for Mr Digby. Waiting to watch Mr Digby. The only man he could talk to about it. If they were talking.

And the split lip? The ringing ears, the closing eye, and the split lip? A final snapshot by way of a coda:

The showers. Chris Humphries and a couple of the gym team in the showers. It is the next day. The day after. Big Ears has arrived late at the track. He has missed Throwaround, and gone straight out on to the track, where he has run and run, round and round the track, alone. The Star Man has not come. The others have boxed and swung and sprung, and Mr Digby has boxed and swung and sprung with them, and Big Ears has run round the track, alone. The others have had Cool Down and Kickaround, and Big Ears has run and run round the track. The others have gone in to shower and change, and Mr Digby has followed them, and still Big Ears has run on in case Mr Digby should change his mind and come out and join him. But he hasn't come, and now the others are finishing their shower. Some have left the showers and are back in the changing room dressing. Only Chris Humphries and a couple of the gym team are still in the showers.

Above the sound of falling water we hear talk from the changing room, and the sudden silence as the door is flung open. We hear the sound of spiked running shoes crossing the changing room floor. Big Ears comes into the showers and plashes across the wet floor to Chris Humphries. He throws himself at him. He yells and throws himself at him, kicking and punching. Chris Humphries is so surprised by the assault that he loses his balance and falls in a scatter of gym team down under his shower. Big Ears throws himself on top of him and hits him again and again. Chris Humphries fights back. He twists and turns under Big Ears and throws him off. Kicking, punching and scratching they roll over and over each other under the shower. Chris Humphries punches Big Ears in the face. He punches and punches him in the face. Big Ears takes Chris Humphries' head by the ears and bangs it on the shower floor. He bangs it and bangs it, and Chris Humphries punches and punches, until Mr Digby arrives.

Mr Digby runs into the showers. Fully clothed he drags Big Ears off Chris Humphries, and holds the two of them apart. His glasses, still snapped at the bridge, still held together by a twist of the Star Man's sticking plaster, are knocked from his nose and swept by the flow of water towards the drain.

Enough, he says. Enough.

Big Ears swipes at Chris Humphries. Chris Humphries swipes at Big Ears. Mr Digby holds them apart.

No, he says. No. That's it. That's enough.

We don't do this, he says. We're The Losers. We don't do this. What are we?

He asks Chris Humphries.

What are we? he says.

Chris Humphries says nothing.

Mr Digby turns to Big Ears.

What are we? he says.

We're The Losers, Big Ears says.

Right, Mr Digby says. Right. And Losers don't fight, right?

He turns to Chris Humphries.

They don't fight, he says. Right?

Right, Chris Humphries says.

So then, Mr Digby says. That's it then, he says. It's over then, he says.

It's over, he says. Right?

All over now, he says.

OK, Chris Humphries says. OK. Yeah. Over.

Tussie Mussie

My friend Price and me, we're talking.

It's lunchtime, we're sitting in the Badge and we're talking. Like every lunchtime, sitting in the Badge and talking. She's telling me all about it.

That's it, she says.

I guess, she says.

She can't make head or tail of it.

Ape, she says.

Ape, that's me. Ape for April. April's me.

Ape, she says, I can't make head or tail of it.

My friend Price and me, we work up The Horseshoes. She works in Valerie's Flowers. I work in Barnard's Territorials, army surplus.

The Horseshoes is this little street off the market. It's got a book shop and a This n' That shop. And it's got Valerie's Flowers. Valerie Payne's Flowers. But it's part of the market, really.

Market and Upmarket, Price says.

Only we're not Upmarket.

Army surplus and a flower stall, Price says. That's Market.

There's a music stall out on the street, and a paint stall, and Henry, who has a coffee stall. This coffee roasting machine and a grinder, and all sorts of bags of coffee, all out on the street.

There's the Badge, which is a Tandoori Restaurant after six o'clock, but during the day it's a cafe.

That's Market.

There's Genghiz outside the bookshop with his pile of old carpets. Just these piles and piles of old Indian and sort of Turkish carpets, and he spreads them out across the pavement. All these colours, out across the pavement.

All weathers, too. Genghiz and his carpets. Summer time and he's sitting barefoot on this pile of carpets. Winter and he's wrapped up in this old afghan fur coat, and he's tied this sheet of plastic out across the pavement, and his old carpets spread out under it.

He's quite a sight, Genghiz. With his eyes and his hair and his beard all cropped close to his face.

That's Market.

All the girls go for Genghiz. But it's still Market.

Price works outside too. I can see her.

Valerie has a shop now. Valerie is Upmarket now. A couple of years ago she moved into Payne's, the old electricians next to the Sherwood's the grocer's. E. J. Sherwood, the sign says, Notable Fruiterers. Upmarket. She calls the shop Valerie Payne.

Price is just based in there. She just gets her flowers from there. She works at Valerie's old stall, on the corner, right next to the market. You can't get much more Market than right next to the market.

I can look up from my desk, in the Territorials — I do cash in the Territorials — and I can see her.

We meet every day. Lunchtime.

We go to the Badge. We sit in the Badge. Talking.

We could meet in the evenings. I used to think we could meet in the evenings. But we never do. We like to get home.

She lives on the other side of town. She lives a bus, then a train, then a bus ride away. I live nearby. I live just ten minutes walk away. We like to get home.

It takes me a long time to finish up at the end of the day.

The flower stall is easy. All Price has to do is bring the

flowers in, and lock up.

She has a manager. A manageress really, but she likes to be called a manager. The Claw. We call her the Claw.

Because she's thin. She has these thin, thin, thin hands. And she beckons.

If you've done something wrong, or if she wants to speak to you – speak with you, she says – she beckons. The lifts this thin, thin, thin hand, like a claw. She sort of lifts it up into this sort of hook, and she twitches it at you.

Chick, chick, she says.

You should hear Price do it. She can do it just exactly. She can do it so you can't tell the difference.

Chick, chick, she says, beckoning. Francesca.

That's Price's name. Francesca.

Francesca, she says. I want to speak with you.

Her name is Merrigan.

We call her The Claw.

She likes to get away early.

The stall isn't supposed to shut till six o'clock, but Valerie isn't there in the afternoons, and The Claw makes Price close it at half five.

At half five Price takes all the flowers from the stall back to the shop. Then all she has to do is close up. Pull down this sort of grill thing over the stall, and lock it. So Merrigan the Claw can go home just after six.

You think she'd let her go. You'd think that once she's brought all the flowers back to the shop and locked the grill, The Claw would let her go. There's no reason I can think off why she shouldn't just go. Merrigan makes her stay till six.

Six o'clock she leaves and heads for the bus. It's a six o'clock bus.

She likes to make it if she can. Sometimes she makes it. You can never tell with buses. She runs.

From the shop to the bus stop, she runs.

It's something to see, Price running.

Sometimes I think the only reason The Claw makes Price stay till six o'clock is to see her running.

I can see them from my desk. Merrigan The Claw. Tibor who does the buying. All peering at the door to see Price running.

I never told her.

They're all thin at the shop. Valerie used to be big, but she's thin now. The Claw is the Claw. Tibor looks like a stick.

Price is not thin.

Price, you know, is the size of a house.

Me, I'm big. There's no getting away from it. I look like a bed sometimes. Sometimes I think I look like one of those big old fashioned inflatable beds. I'm big. But Price is the size of a house.

I have to stay till half six.

I have to cash up.

There's this complicated way I have to cash up, with all sorts of separate columns for all sorts of credit cards, and a different section for cash and cheques, and more often than not it doesn't all balance up and I have to do it again.

And then there's the stock check, and the reordering. And shelving. I'm lucky if I get away by seven.

And then I like to get home.

Sometimes I think I should like to talk.

Sometimes I think I should like to stop and talk.

But it's good to get home.

So we meet at lunchtime, my friend Price and me. We meet lunchtimes at the Badge. And we talk.

Bloody talking.

So anyway. She can't make head or tail of it.

Ape, she says, that's it. That's all there is to it. I can't make head or tail of it.

I've got a headache.

She's pushed her plate back. She's had pork chops and onion gravy and a portion of bubble. Me, I've had egg, bacon, sausage and chips.

They do a good chip at the Badge. Big cuts of potato, fried just right, just crisp and dry in beef dripping. Just right. They do a good bubble too. It's Price's turn for the bubble. I'm still eating my egg, bacon, sausage and chips. I'm eating slow today. I've got a headache.

Ape, she says. I don't know what to make of it.

She's holding her tea. She's got her hands round that mug of tea, and she's holding on to it.

Tell me what you make of it, she says.

She has big hands. Her fingers round the mug, they look like sausages. They're not pretty, Price's fingers.

You'd think, wouldn't you? You'd think it was pretty, working in a flower shop. All those flowers, you'd think it was pretty. It's not pretty. It's cold and it's wet. It's buckets and chicken wire. It's out in all weathers on the stall. It's cold water. Price's fingers, they're chapped and cracked and red, and there's a cake of dirt under her fingernails.

There's this customer, she says.

It's what we talk about. Customers. You wouldn't believe what customers can do. The things customers can do.

He's sick, I think, she says.

Like I say, customers. You wouldn't believe what they do. There's this kilt. In the Territorials we've got this kilt. It's not a big kilt. It's about the smallest kilt you can get, but we hang it up anyway, and people ask to try it on.

Hunting Stewart tartan it is. It looks good up there on its hanger, and a whole lot of people ask to try it on. I tell them it's too small. It's very small, I say. You can't get the big ones.

There's this man. This customer. He comes in but he doesn't buy. He sort of hangs around. He looks at this and that. Sometimes you think he's going to speak. Ask the price of this. Can he try on that? He never does.

Then we got the kilt. I saw him looking at it. He looked and looked, and after he went away, about half an hour after he went away, we got this phone call: Did we have any kilts?

I said yes, we had one, but it was only a small one. We never got big ones. He'd have to wait a long time if he wanted a big one.

I knew it was him. He didn't say. I just knew.

Next day there he was back, looking at the kilt.

You can tell when they're going to lift stuff. They hang around. They look this way and that. You can tell. I knew he was going to try and lift it. The kilt. I kept an eye on him.

I called in Phyllida from the warehouse, and she came and kept an eye on him. She came and stood near him.

Only you can't keep an eye all the time. You've got a shop to run, and come six o'clock it can get busy, what with the closing rush and all. And Phyllida has things to do in the warehouse, so we got distracted sort of. And come two minutes to six, there he is heading for the door, and no sign of the kilt.

I buzz for Phyllida and I shove round the counter to head him off. I get him up against the wall, and Phyllida comes and talks to him.

I'm sorry, she says. But I'm going to have to see under the coat.

He's wearing this coat. This khaki camouflage coat.

Yeah, I say. Come on. Show us what you've got under the coat.

He doesn't look so comfortable. He looks all shifty.

It's no good, Phyllida says. I've got to insist. I've got to see under that coat.

He's all sort of looking at his feet, but he opens the coat.

I see it first, then Phyllida sees it.

Oh for God's sake, she says.

It's sticking out of his trousers. These khaki camouflage

trousers, like his coat, and it's sticking out of them.

Well, we're just about to close, Phyllida says. And you know what? I suggest you do too.

And she laughs.

We both laugh.

Bloody laughing.

So anyway. He's still looking at his feet. He goes away. He doesn't do up his coat, but he goes away.

Phyllida finds the kilt. It's fallen off it's hanger. It's down under the rack.

I tell you. Customers.

I'm pretty sure, Price says.

A bit maybe, she says.

He just doesn't look well, she says. You know.

I'm fiddling with my food. It's gone cold. All sort of bacon fat and cold egg yolk. Half a sausage and some chips. Not so good cold, the chips.

I look at my fingers round the fork. They look, I'm thinking, like sausages as well. Like fat white sausages. Like those big white german sausages.

He's got this cough, she says.

I don't want to talk about customers. Sometimes, you know, they can make you sick, customers.

And I've got this headache. The back of my head aches. Those two lobe things at the back, at the bottom. They ache.

What about The Claw? I say.

That's the other thing we talk about. Customers and The Claw.

Like when she got this raise. Price. She'd been there three years, and Valerie gave her this raise. And she told Tibor about it.

How much do you get then? he asked her, and she told him, I get four pounds an hour. I used to get three, but I got this raise..

And after lunch there she was on her stall, and The Claw comes out.

Chick, chick, she says.

I want to speak with you, she says.

And she beckons.

Well really, she says.

Francesca, she says. You didn't ought to have done that.

That's what she's always saying, Price says. All tight-lipped and genteel. All stout-mouthed, Price says. You didn't ought to have done that.

Done what? Price says.

Told Tibor, she says. What you earn. You earn more than he does. And now he knows. You didn't ought to have done that.

You should have heard her. She's got The Claw to the life. You should hear her.

I'd rather talk about The Claw.

It doesn't do any good.

Because, oh yeah, she says. I didn't tell you. She was pissed off today. Boy was she pissed off today. He asked for me.

She was at the stall, she says.

She does the stall too sometimes, The Claw. She doesn't like it, but sometimes Valerie's in the shop, and when Valerie's in the shop she likes The Claw to go out on the stall.

And there he is at the stall. And The Claw goes up to him, all stout-mouthed and genteel.

Can I help you? she says.

Oh no, he says. It's all right. It's your colleague I've come to see.

You should have seen her face, she says. If looks could kill. Her lips, they just crimped, she says. And Chick, chick, she said. And she beckoned. I'm going to be in for it. You wait. I get back from lunch, you just wait.

She laughs.

She hugs her mug. Her sausage fingers round her mug.

He's not so young, she says.

Kind of short, she says, you know. Kind of not too clean.

I'm still fiddling with my food.

He could do with a shave, she says.

I saw this film once. This horror film. This man had on this sort of mask. This helmet. And it got tighter and tighter round his head. That's what my head feels like. Like these bands at the back of my head, getting tighter and tighter.

He likes my flowers, she says.

Valerie's pretty strict about her flowers. At Valerie's it's Valerie who does the flowers. Tibor sometimes, when Valerie's away. Sometimes The Claw, but she can't do it. She knows she can't do it. I don't arrange, she says. I manage. I manage very well, she says. I don't arrange.

Only one day Price was talking.

She'd found this idea. She's been reading and she'd found this idea. Tussie Mussie.

Tussie bloody Mussie.

It's a sort of nosegay, she said. This sort of cottage garden nosegay.

You take ordinary flowers and things, she said. Like the sort of things you'd find in an old-fashioned cottage garden. Like lowly things, you know, and you make a nosegay. Like lavender, you know. And rosemary. And a bit of box. Some snowdrops. A jonquil. A primrose. Some catkins. Some peach blossom. A bit of birch. Some ivy maybe. Ordinary things.

And Valerie heard. And she liked it.

They're pretty too. You should see them. Price, you know, she's got the gift. These grayish, brownish, greenish nosegay things, with a bit of colour from the flowers. You should see them.

So Valerie lets her make them up, and sell them on the stall. Not in the shop. They're a bit Market for the shop. But they look good on the stall. People like them on the stall.

The Claw was furious. You should have seen The Claw. She was just furious.

And he likes them, she says.

He looked at them, she says. And he liked them. And he looked at the label.

Tussie Mussie? he says. What's Tussie Mussie?

It's what they are, I say. I don't know what it means. Just Tussie Mussie. It's what they are.

He coughs.

I said, she says, he has this cough.

Tussie Mussie, he says. I like that. It sounds like a cough.

He coughs again.

Tussie Mussie.

And it does, she says. It does, Ape, you know.

Ape, that's me. Ape for April.

Tussie Mussie, she says. It sounds like a cough.

And that's it, she says. I guess. That's it.

That's it? I say.

That's what? I say. What's it?

I can feel my eyes bulge. This guy in the film. The helmet got tighter and tighter, and his eyes bulged and bulged. Till they fell out. I can feel my eyes bulging and bulging. And you know, you bulge the way I do. I'm big, I told you. You're big the way I am, you don't want your eyes to bulge too.

I got this feeling, she says.

What feeling? I say.

I can see her hands round the mug. I can see what she's going to do. She's going to let go of the mug and she's going to reach out and touch me. She's going to reach out and put her hand on me. On mine.

I don't know, she says. Just this feeling.

I put my hands in my lap. I'm not having that. She can do what she wants, but I'm not having that.

I don't know what to make of it, she says.

She lets go of her mug.

I can't make head or tail of it, she says.

This feeling, Ape, she says.

Ape for April. That's me.

What do you make of it, Ape? she says.

And I'm not having it. I sit with my hands in my lap. I just sit looking at my hands in my lap.

Ape? she says.

I can't tell you how much my head aches. I just can't tell you how much my head aches. I wait for her to go.

I can tell when it's the end of something. I just wait for her to go.

I look and look at my hands in my lap.

When I look up she's gone.

When I look up I can see her, gone. I can see her walking down the street. Away down the street, down The Horseshoes. I can see her.

She's walking past the stationers and the This n' That shop. She's walking past the pet shop (Market) and the paint shop (Upmarket). Past Henry and the coffee stall. Past the bookshop. Past Genghiz and his carpets and his colours all spilling out across the pavement. Past Genghiz with his eyes, and his hair, and his teeth, and his throaty, smoky smell. All the girls go for Genghiz. And on into Valerie's. Valerie Payne's. Opposite Barnard's Territorials.

My friend Price.

That's it. I guess.

The Lie

Greg Hamill told the lie at the beginning of the summer.

They were sitting, James Carver and he, in a bar on the Bayswater Road. It was a Wednesday, and lunch time. Greg Hamill was complaining.

I don't know why, he said, I keep coming to this place. It's not as if anything happens.

Oh I don't know, James Carver said. That one's not bad. The one in blue. The one just drinking his pint. He's not bad.

No, Greg Hamill said. Not for me. Too tall. Too wide. I don't like the moustache.

The man in blue put down his pint and leaned on the bar. He looked straight at Greg Hamill and smiled. Greg Hamill looked at his beer.

American I would say, James Carver said. Judging by the jeans. And the teeth.

Greg Hamill looked up from his beer. The man in blue smiled again, picked up his drink, and crossed to sit next to Greg Hamill.

From the conversation that followed these are some of the facts that emerged:

The man in blue was called Paul, Paul Usher, from Cleveland, Ohio, an architecture student from UCLA, over here for four weeks as part of his summer vacation.

James Carver and Greg Hamill had travelled quite a bit too. In fact they were going to San Francisco at the end of July, to stay with James Carver's uncle.

The man in blue was staying in a small hotel just round

the corner.

Greg Hamill found the man in blue tall, but no longer too tall. Wide, but not too wide. Nor was his moustache insuperably objectionable.

Also during this conversation Greg Hamill told the lie. James Carver didn't notice. It was just one sentence among many.

Funny, isn't it? James Carver said, while the man in blue was at the bar buying a round of drinks. The way people become more attractive the more available they are.

After the next drink James Carver excused himself, and went to sit at the other end of the room. Greg Hamill and the man in blue talked till closing time, then went round the corner to the man in blue's hotel.

Over the next few days things proceeded according to their pattern: Greg Hamill and the man in blue ran into each other on the street, bumped into each other in bars, and smiled at their good fortune. At the end of the first week they made a date, missed each other, and met again after a flurry of phone calls. By the end of the second week they were seeing each other every day.

The man in blue shaved off his moustache.

On the morning of the Monday of the third week the lie surfaced in a manner that startled Greg Hamill considerably. He choked on his morning coffee, hung up as naturally as possible on the man in blue, and went so hurriedly to see James Carver that he left a cigarette burning in the ashtray.

James Carver opened the door in his dressing gown.

I've got to talk to you, Greg Hamill said.

James Carver made coffee while Greg Hamill fidgeted on his stool and bit his fingernails. When the coffee was made James Carver sat down opposite Greg Hamill and lit a cigarette.

All right, he said. Go ahead.

I can't, Greg Hamill said. I can't tell you.

And he got off his stool and left. James Carver finished his cigarette and drank both cups of coffee. It was Friday morning before he heard from Greg Hamill again.

I'm sorry, Greg Hamill said. I've got to see you. I've got to talk to you. I don't know what to do.

They met at the Round Pond and walked through Kensington Gardens.

Isn't it awful, Greg Hamill said. When you're a reasonably honest and reliable person. But you sometimes lie a little.

James Carver agreed that it was awful.

I mean. Greg Hamill said. You don't get anything for nothing in this life. So you just pretend to have a bit more to give than you really have, and there you are.

Maybe, James Carver said. If you just told me what you were talking about.

It's Paul, Greg Hamill said. He's leaving next Friday. He's bought a ticket for Hawaii.

James Carver waited.

He's always wanted to go, Greg Hamill said. And now he's going back to California via Hawaii. He's going to stay with friends of mine.

You haven't, James Carver said, got any friends in Hawaii. You haven't even been to Hawaii.

I said I did, Greg Hamill said. That day in the pub, when we first met. I said I did. I don't know what to do. The only person I know from Hawaii is a trick I met here in London years ago. Paul found his name in my address book. I just embroidered a bit. I said we were old friends.

I see, James Carver said.

I was just showing off, that's all, Greg Hamill said. Things just built up and up. They got out of hand. You know how it is. He thinks we're practically best friends. He thinks I've written, for God's sake, to say he's coming. What on earth am I going to do?

You could always forget it, James Carver said. After all, we're going away ourselves in two weeks.

I thought of that, Greg Hamill said. But his ticket is for San Francisco. He says he's coming to see us after he's been to Hawaii.

Oh dear, James Carver said.

I thought I could say we were only going to be in San Francisco for a few days, Greg Hamill said. Then we're going to see your uncle who lives out of town somewhere. I don't know where.

Maybe, James Carver said, I ought to be unavailable for a few days. If you think it will work.

Isn't it a mess? Greg Hamill said. I can't eat. I can't sleep. I feel sick all the time.

You could say, James Carver said, that they were an item, these friends of yours. They wrote to you to say they've split up. And they've moved. And they don't want to see anyone.

I could just not answer the phone, Greg Hamill said.

Or you could tell the truth, James Carver said. You could say that you made it all up.

Oh God, Greg Hamill said. The first decent person I meet in an age, and I have to go and mess it up.

The next Friday Greg Hamill and James Carver went to see the man in blue off at Heathrow. James Carver, who had been unavailable for the week, wondered where they were seeing him off to, but felt it would be indiscreet to ask.

At the check-in the man in blue talked about how much he was looking forward to Hawaii. He had always wanted to go Hawaii, and here he was, going.

James Carver looked at Greg Hamill, But Greg Hamill was busy with the man in blue's bags.

While they waited for the flight they sat over coffees and Danish pastries, and James Carver prattled of neutral matters.

Greg Hamill sniffed and looked unhappy, which may or may not have been because, as he said, he hated goodbyes, even temporary ones.

At the word Temporary James Carver looked up and tried and failed again to catch Greg Hamill's eye.

When the flight was called they went and stood outside the departure lounge. The man in blue shook James Carver's hand, and kissed Greg Hamill, and said he would see them both soon, in San Francisco. Again James Carver tried to catch Greg Hamill's eye, but Greg Hamill was brushing away a tear, and James Carver had to turn away.

The man in blue kissed Greg Hamill again and told him not to be sad. They would see each other again, real soon. Then he disappeared into the departure lounge.

This time James Carver did manage to catch Greg Hamill's eye. He decided not to say anything.

Comp'ny

I had this cat.

We had this cat. She bought this cat. L did.

I got home from work one day and there it was, this cat. L had seen this notice on the notice board at work. She works as a receptionist at the local health centre. Please save the life of a cat, the notice said. If I can't find a new home for my cat, the notice said, it will have to be put down. So she bought it. The cat. And she brought it home. I got home from work – I work in an office, for the Ministry of Defence, as a clerical officer; it's a fair way away, I get home tired – and there it was. This skinny grey cat. A sort of brindled grey. Tabby only grey.

We lived in a basement.

She loved it. The cat. She really loved it. She spoiled it rotten. It lived in the lap of luxury, that cat. She bought it a special basket, only it didn't sleep in it. A big wicker basket with a cushion, and it wouldn't have anything to do with it. It sat on a chair. As far as I could see it spent all day sitting on this chair. This sort of upholstered dining chair I'd found in the market. I find a lot of stuff in the market. I liked that chair. I used it to sit on when I sat at the table. When I was sitting on it, and I always had to push the cat off to sit on it, the cat sat on the bed.

It slept on the bed too. Every night when we went to bed the cat would join us. It would curl up between us. It would circle and trample and pump with its feet till it got a comfortable space, and sometimes I would wake up and find it sleeping across my feet. If it did that, and I knew L was asleep, I would kick it off.

The window was left open for it all day, so it could nip in and out of the garden. It was a sash window, and the sash was broken. The only way it could be kept open was if you propped it open with a stick. I sawed a piece off an old broom handle and L left the window propped open with that. Rain or shine the window was left open. I would come back and find the windowsill all wet more often that not, and muddy paw prints drying off over everything.

The window was left open for it all night too. If you wanted to close the window you had to make sure it was in. You had to shake a packet of chocolate cat munchies and it would come running in to eat and you could close the window. If you didn't do that it would scratch on the window some time during the night till it woke you up and you let it in. Sometimes it would scratch on the window to wake you up to let it out. L was a heavy sleeper. She would sleep through all the scratchings. It was me who woke up.

She bought it toys. She would come home day after day with a little parcel which the cat would unwrap. You should have seen that cat unwrap a parcel. Piles of little furry toys with bells on, and the cat would slobber over them and claw them to pieces and leave wet bits of them where you didn't want to find them. And things to chew, and things to scratch. It went off to the cat parlour every month to have its claws clipped, and its ears seen to. She bought it a velvet collar with a little silver disc with its name on.

And the food. She spent a fortune on food. And never a tin of cat food did she buy. Fresh fish. Chicken breast. Chopped liver. Rabbit. The cat ate better than I did. And the fuss. If the cat was off its food – and you wouldn't believe the number of times it would turn up its nose at a sliver of salmon, a prawn or two, or a saucer of cream – little tempting morsels of some-thing else would be dangled at it till it deigned to eat.

She loved it. L. That cat.

And it loved her. She would stroke it and stroke it, and fuss over it and fuss over it, and it would squirm and stretch and purr. It would writhe round her legs and head-butt her, all the time purr, purr, purr, enough to make your head ache.

It didn't love me. Me it ignored. L would scoop it up on to her lap in the evening when we were watching television and it would sit there purring. If I tried to pick it up it would go all stiff and wriggle away. If I persisted and picked it up and put it on my lap and tried to stroke it, it would scratch my leg and jump off. I shouldn't mind, L said. After all it wasn't my cat. It was her cat. It was a one man cat.

Sometimes it would run off. I would come home from the office every now and again, and there would be L, all frantic. No cat. She'd looked everywhere. She'd been out in the garden calling. She'd been up and down the street calling. What was she going to do? What was I going to do? And I would have to go out into the garden and call. I would have to go up and down the street calling. The cat was called Tutti. Don't ask why. I don't know why. She called it Tutti. And if you want to feel a bloody fool, try standing in the garden for half an hour, try walking up and down the street, calling out, Tutti, Tutti. Knowing damn well it wasn't going to do any good. God knows what good she thought it was going to do. It never did any good. The cat came back when the cat chose to come back. We'd have gone to bed usually, L all sulky and upset and not able to sleep, and I'd be just dropping off, and there would be this scratching at the window. The cat back as if nothing had happened. Tearful reunion. She loved that cat.

Only she can't have loved it as much as I thought, because when she left she left it with me.

I don't know why she left. I didn't ask. You didn't know L. Once she had made her mind up, there was no point in asking. I spent a lot of time thinking about it. She didn't say. It had always been a temporary arrangement, is all she said. I knew it had always been a temporary arrangement, is what she said. Well yes, I thought. I suppose. But it was a temporary arrangement that had gone on for eleven years. I mean, if you look at it like that, what isn't a temporary arrangement?

I thought about it a lot. I ended up thinking that I wasn't surprised. I'm no catch, basically, I thought. In the end, I thought, it was more or less less of a surprise that she moved out than that she moved in in the first place. Let alone spent so long. That's what I ended up thinking.

I was surprised, though, that she left the cat.

I didn't like the cat.

Even when L was there I didn't like the cat. It was a messy cat. And after she had gone, after I couldn't see her playing with the cat any more, and the cat writhing round her legs and head-butting her, and purring, purring, I didn't like it a lot more.

After she'd gone, the cat lost its privileges. No more presents. Those old toys, they got thrown out. No more chocolate cat munchies. No more trips to the parlour for nail clipping and ear cleaning. You wouldn't believe how much that stuff costs.

It didn't sleep on the bed any more. I don't know if it slept in its basket or not. I expect it slept on my dining chair, to judge by the amount of cat hair I had to brush off the thing every day. Once I got to the office and everyone was laughing at me. I was going round with this pad of cat fur on the seat of my trousers, picked up from my dining chair. One thing I do know, it didn't sleep on my bed.

And it didn't go out of the window day and night either. I shut the window when I left in the morning, and the cat spent the day in or out, depending on where it was when I shut the window. I shut it at night too. I put plugs in my ears, and if the cat scratched and scratched to go in or out I didn't hear it.

And the dirt. That cat was dirty. I was lying on my bed one evening, reading, and the window was open, and I saw the cat jump in. It was a sunny evening and I could see the air round the cat. It was full of a cloud of dust and shed hairs that the cat was dragging around with it.

The food stopped too. All that special food. That cat got a new dish. It got a blue plastic dish with two compartments in it. And that dish got washed and filled once a day, one compartment with water, and one compartment with Kit-E-Kat. If it didn't eat what I gave it I figured it wasn't hungry.

And it didn't like me. I don't know, maybe if it had liked me I could have liked it more. But it didn't. It still wouldn't even let me pick it up.

It broke my stuff. I had some nice stuff. Some pots and things I'd found in the market. I find a lot of stuff in the market. You wouldn't believe what you can find in the market if you know how to look. And the cat broke them. One after the other the cat broke them. I would come home from the office, and there would be something else, broken.

It threw up all over everything. I would find these sodden wads of thrown-up fur all over the place. I'd find them on the furniture and in the kitchen. Once I found one on the stove. Once I left some important papers from work out on my desk and I found one on them.

One thing, though, really got on my nerves. I mean, the cat didn't like me, right? And it watched me all the time. Whatever I did it watched me. And every time I moved it jumped up and ran to its food bowl. All the time. Every time I moved. Morning or evening. Day or night. Whether the food bowl was full or empty. Every time I moved, that cat ran to the food bowl. And mewed. And shook. And trembled its tail. That really got on my nerves.

And when it ran off, and it still ran off, sometimes it ran off for days on end, I didn't chase it. I didn't go out in the garden and call it. I didn't go up and down the street calling it. When it ran off I was relieved. I hoped it wouldn't come back.

It always came back though.

That cat just couldn't stay away.

I decided to get rid of it. I put up this notice in the office. Please save the life of a cat, the notice said. If I can't find a new home for my cat, it will have to be put down.

We lived in this basement.

I lived in this garden flat, just round the corner from the market. I used to rent it, then I bought it. A year or two before L moved in I bought it. I got this endowment mortgage. I'm well into the payments now.

It's a double-fronted house. It has two basements. Violet lived in the other basement. Florrie lived on the ground floor right. And the rest of the house was a maisonette. The garden was mine.

I'm no good at gardens. Whatever the opposite of green fingers are, I have them. What I did was, I made it low maintenance. I shingled it all over, and put up a couple of old statues I found in the market, and some plants in pots which you can replace when they die. You walked out of the back door into this sort of area, where we kept our bikes, then up some ivied old steps to the shingled garden. It had some roses in a corner, and a barbecue, but mostly it was just shingle. It looked all right.

The cat liked it too. The cat thought the shingle was cat litter. You wouldn't believe the amount of mess a cat can leave. I had to rake it up. I bought this stuff you could pour over it to stop the cat, but L wouldn't let me use it. Poor Tutti, she said. Why shouldn't she use the garden if she wants. It's her garden too, she said. I raked it up.

It was a big maisonette. It had this huge spiral staircase running up from the door on the ground floor to the roof terrace on the top. The central column of the spiral staircase ended in our flat. Whenever anyone went up and down the spiral staircase you could hear their footsteps sound down this metal column in the hall of our flat. This woman called Jane lived in it, and Marshall Dillon, her husband, and their daughter, Ribbon.

Jane was this doctor's daughter from Surrey. She was doing some sort of course at the local college. Marshall Dillon was the local drugs dealer. Ribbon was just a little girl. I caught her one day, throwing stones out of the back window at the cat.

It was quite an area for drugs. Sometimes you couldn't take a step outside your front door without someone hissing at you for drugs. You want dope, man? You want hash, man? L didn't like it. She never got used to it. I used to say, All you have to do is smile and say no. But she didn't like it. Once she spoke to one of them. Are you addressing me? she said. It didn't work. They just laughed. This man just looked at her, and called out, Hey, you hear what this white woman say to me? She say, You addressing me? And everyone laughed.

Marshall Dillon supplied the drugs. He used to give parties. Once when we got home we found this woman, this girl really, lying on our bed. She got up when we came in, and said, You're not going to believe this. I've been to this party, she said. Upstairs. And I didn't like it. So I climbed out of the window and into the garden. And in through your window, only your door was locked and I couldn't get out.

Soon after that Marshall Dillon went away. There was this story. That Jane wrote this thesis for her course. On drugs. On the spread and influence of drugs in a local community. And that she used all sorts of examples from Marshall Dillon's work. Only the college gave the thesis to the police, and they used it as evidence against Marshall Dillon. I don't know if it's true.

I do know that I came home one day and saw Marshall

Dillon loading all sorts of furniture and stuff on to a lorry. And the next time I saw Jane she was in the local store, buying ice. My fridge has gone, she said. Well, it's been stolen, actually. Marshall Dillon had loaded up this lorry with everything in the flat, carpets, shelves, everything, and gone.

Which lets you know what sort of area it was. It wasn't the sort of area you wanted to run up and down the street in, calling, Tutti! Tutti!

Violet and Florrie were two old women. L liked old women. Violetta, she called them, and Florence. Pronounced in the French way. Florence. Don't ask me why. Not to their face, of course. Inside every old woman, she said, is the pretty little girl she used to be.

Florrie lived upstairs. You would have been hard put to it, I thought, to think of a pretty little girl inside Florrie. She was the grandmother of the people who ran the fruit and vegetable stall round the corner in the market. And you really couldn't call her nice. I thought she was dirty, actually, and rude. She had this wrinkled face and hands, and all this dirt in the wrinkles. A lot of the time she was drunk. She used to come knocking on our door, asking for things. Could she just use our phone? Could she just use our loo? Did we have any cigarettes, she'd run out? I was all for saying no. But I wasn't allowed to. We should be kind, L said. We were going to be old ourselves one day.

She used to get drunk and shout, Florrie. Quite often we'd hear her. Often in the middle of the night. Yelling. The walls of the house were thin. You could hear the people next door. You could hear Marshall Dillon's parties. You could hear Jane on the phone. You could hear Ribbon crying, and Florrie yelling. She would get falling over drunk, and yell. Violet used to worry. She was scared, she said one day to L. She was sure that Florrie, who smoked, was going to get drunk once too often, and burn the place down. You could hear Violet through the wall too. Not often. She had this friend. This man friend. And every now and again you could hear her shouting at him to get out. You're all the same, you'd hear. You men. You only want one thing, you men. L loved that.

One day, in the rain, there was this family sheltering in our porch. This Asian family. This Indian woman and two girls, all in saris, keeping out of the rain in our porch. And you should have heard Florrie yelling at them. Get out of here, she yelled. You dirty Pakis. Get away from my door. They tried to say that they were only sheltering from the rain, but she went in and got a broom, and drove them away. We changed towards Florrie after that. Or L did. The next time Florrie came knocking on our door after that, she got sent away. She'd locked herself out, and she wanted us to let her in. I'll tell you what, she got told. You just stay there and I'll call your grandson. You can ask him to come and help you. Oh no, Florrie said. I don't want to disturb him. The next time she came we didn't answer the door.

Violet lived in the basement next to ours.

You could tell the time by Violet. Every day at half past ten exactly she walked past our window on her way to the pub. And every day at ten past three exactly she and her man friend walked back past it on their way back. And again after dinner. Eight o'clock to the pub, eleven o'clock back. It wasn't a pub we used so we never saw them in there. I only once saw her in a pub. It wasn't her local one, and it was after her man friend died, but I expect it was much the same. She sat by herself with a half of stout, and all this noise, pub noise, just went on round her.

It was sad when he died. The man friend. He was a local business man. He had this electrician's shop just off the market, which we never used. I tried to use it once when my hoover broke, but it wasn't his brand of hoover so I had to go somewhere else. He retired just after he took up with Violet, and a couple of years later he died. Afterwards Violet stopped going to the pub for a while, and then started up again, by herself. And once we saw her in Barker's tea rooms, sitting by herself over a cup of tea. We nodded and waved, but she didn't seem to want to talk.

The Queen Mother without teeth we called her then. L called her. She used to talk to her. I never really talked to her. She had this old feathered hat, which she always wore, and this full gray coat, and she often went out without her teeth.

She liked the cat. It was how we found out where the cat went when it went off. Some of the times it went off. Once we met her on the street as we were going out, and she came up to us and talked to us about the cat. She got the name wrong.

That Tootsie, she said. She liked that Tootsie. She'd never seen a cat that liked its food like that Tootsie. She fed her every now and then. She called her in to keep her company every now and again. Comp'ny she said. She hoped we didn't mind. It was just after her man friend died. She was wearing her feathered hat and her full gray coat, and she didn't have her teeth in. We said we didn't mind.

That Tootsie, she said. She's a cat. I like that Tootsie.

She would have been the right person to take the cat on, I used to think sometimes. But of course it wasn't possible. And next door was too close really, anyway. The cat would never have stayed away.

She came knocking on our door on the Sunday morning.

We were all asleep. L, me and the cat. I was dozing mainly. The sun shines straight in the window on a summer morning, and straight into my eyes. Sometimes I get up to pull the curtains. Sometimes I'm just too lazy, and I turn away and doze. I was dozing when she came knocking, so it was me who went and opened the door.

She was ever so sorry, she said.

It was Violet. In her feathered hat and full gray coat, with her teeth in.

She was sorry to disturb us, she said. She hadn't wanted to disturb us, but there was something going on upstairs. She was sure there was something going on upstairs. She was worried. Could we come and look?

The cat came out of the bedroom and ran towards her. It writhed round her legs and head-butted her.

There's this smell, she said. In the bathroom. And it's hot.

I went next door. All in my dressing gown and slippers, I went round to her flat. It was the first time I'd been into her flat. She hadn't done much to the place. It was empty, more or less. A few sticks of furniture. No carpet. Nothing on the walls, only this picture in the sitting room. This wedding picture of the Prince and Princess of Wales, cut out of some magazine and pinned to the wall. The paper all yellow and torn at the edges, and the colours all fading.

I went into the bathroom. Her flat is a mirror image of mine, so I knew straightaway where everything was. There was this smell of burning and the ceiling was hot. There was smoke coming out of the ventilator shaft, and if you listened you could hear this crackling and spitting from upstairs.

I went back to the front room, where Violet still was.

I didn't want to disturb you, she said. I've been waiting. I noticed a funny smell last night, but I didn't want to wake you up.

You'd better get your things, I said. I'm going to call the fire brigade.

L was still asleep when I got back next door. The cat was curled up next to her in the sunlight. The phone is by the bed. I woke her up and told her to call the fire brigade, and went back to Violet.

Violet hadn't got her things. She was in the bathroom, looking up at the ceiling. As I came in the ceiling cracked and all this plaster came down, followed by all these sparks, and smoke. I took her back to the sitting room, and helped her get her things. She didn't have much. She just wanted her handbag, really. Only she couldn't remember where it was, and I had to find it. It was in her bedroom. You could tell from the bed that she hadn't gone to sleep. She had sat up all night, worried by the smell from upstairs.

I gave her her bag and took her out. I wanted to take her into my flat, but she wouldn't come. She stood on the pavement and looked at her flat. The whole place looked all right to me, as if nothing was happening. Florrie's curtains were drawn, and you couldn't see anything.

Well, I said. It looks as if she's finally done it.

L came out, with the cat, and this chair and this blanket. She sat Violet down in the chair and wrapped her in this blanket. And the cat jumped up and sat on her lap. L sent me in to make a cup of tea. Hot, sweet tea, she said. By the time I came back with the tea the fire brigade had arrived, Florrie's window had cracked in the heat and a great piece of glass fallen out, and thick, black smoke was pouring out of the hole. The firemen were going in and out of the building, her place, and Violet's, and soon the smoke started pouring out of Violet's door. There was no one in upstairs, apparently. Jane and Ribbon were spending the weekend back in Surrey, I guessed.

Violet sat on her chair, wrapped in her blanket, stroking the cat, and watched. She didn't seem to take much in. She just sat there. Once she opened her handbag to look inside. She drank her tea. Most of the time she just stroked the cat.

Then the head fireman came up and whispered could we take her in now, please. We're going to have to take the body out now, he said, and it would be better if the old lady wasn't there to see.

It was the first time it had occurred to me that there might be a body.

He went up to Violet and put his hand on her shoulder.

Come on now, love, he said. You'd better go in now, love, he said.

Violet didn't move. She didn't move until L went up to her with another cup of tea.

Come on, Mrs Rogers, L said. We'd better go in now. You just come in and sit down on the sofa, and have another cup of tea.

She went in then, and they brought the body out.

I don't like to think of this next bit. Florrie must have been drunk, the fireman said. She must have been drunk and fallen asleep in her chair. And she must have dropped her cigarette down the chair. Death traps, those old chairs, he said. They'd found her body in the bathroom. She must have fallen asleep, he said, and woken up when the burning chair burnt her legs. They take a long time to go, those chairs, he said. But when they go that's it. They go. And she must have crawled to the bathroom to get some cold water to put on her legs. And that's where the smoke got her. He said.

They carried her out under a blanket. I could see why they'd made us take Violet in. Even under the blanket you could see that the body was all twisted and wouldn't lie down properly.

You couldn't call her nice, but I don't like to think of that.

Violet sat on the sofa in our living room. The cat followed her in and sat on her lap.

We watched from the window. You wouldn't believe how long it takes to put out a fire. Even a small one like this one. Not much was burnt, apparently. The chair, of course, and the floor between the two flats. The worst thing was the smoke. Both flats were full of it. And after everything is out they have to wait to see that nothing has spread anywhere. We made everyone cups of tea. We used every cup in the place. We set up this sort of tea shuttle service. And we gave everyone a glass of sherry before they left.

And of course, when they'd all gone, there was nowhere for Violet to go. It hadn't occurred to me that there wouldn't be anywhere for her to go. She sat on our sofa until a policeman came in and asked her if she had anywhere to go.

So, love, he said. OK, Love. We'd better get you off then.

Violet looked at him and didn't say anything. Then she looked at L.

Mrs Rogers, L said. He's asking if there's anywhere you can go.

I want to go home, Violet said.

Well, yes, love, the policeman said. Don't we all? But you'll have to go somewhere else for the moment, won't you?

Won't you, love? he said.

Violet looked at L again. The cat was sitting in her lap and she was stroking it. It was purring and pumping with its feet.

Mrs Rogers, L said. It will be a while before you can go back, you know. The place will be a mess. They'll have to do it up again. Is there anywhere you can go in the meantime?

Oh no, Violet said. I'm going home.

The policeman took out his notebook.

How old are you then, love? he said.

L sat down next to Violet on the sofa.

Mrs Rogers, she said. He needs to know how old you are.

Violet smiled.

This will surprise you, she said. I'm eighty. I was eighty last November. I'm eighty.

The policeman wrote in his notebook.

And there isn't anywhere you can go? he said.

L took Mrs Violet's hand. Violet took it away again, and stroked the cat.

Is there anyone? L said. Any family maybe.

Well there was someone, Violet said. You knew him, didn't you? My gentleman friend. You met him. There was him.

He used to come and see me all the time, she said. You

know how it is. Comp'ny. You need a bit of comp'ny. But he died.

The policeman wrote in his notebook.

Anyone else? he said.

Violet looked at L.

There's my sister, she said. But we don't talk. We haven't talked. Oh for years. Not for years.

The policeman snapped his notebook shut.

Well then, love, he said. Saint Stephen's it is then.

Saint Stephen's is the local old people's home. It's this old redbrick building with towers and all sorts of Gothic stuff, just round the corner on the other side of the market.

Violet crossed her arms on the sofa. The cat stopped purring and jumped off her lap.

I'm not going, she said.

Come on then, love, the policeman said.

I'm not going there, Violet said. You won't get me going there.

And she wouldn't move. The policeman took her by the arm, but she wouldn't move.

Come on, love, the policeman said. You can't stay here, you know.

I won't go, Violet said. I won't go there. I won't.

I didn't know what to do. I mean, the policeman was right, she couldn't stay here. The policeman looked at me. He didn't know what to do either. He could hardly just pick her up and carry her off if she didn't want to go. L knew what to do.

She sat back on the sofa.

Oh well, she said. You'll just have to stay here then.

I looked at her hard. She didn't look at me.

It's a pity though, she said.

I mean, she said. When you think about it. It's a pity to miss it. There will be men there. Just think of all the men there.

Violet reached for her handbag.

I should think, L said, it would be quite fun there. Wouldn't you? Don't you think all those people would be fun?

Violet went with the policeman.

I did the washing up after they'd gone. You wouldn't believe all the washing up. Every cup in the place. A whole pile of sherry glasses. I was a bit worried for a while. I mean, what if the fire started up again? But then I thought, No, it wouldn't. The firemen wouldn't have all gone away if it was going to start up again, would they? I dried everything up, and I put it all away. You wouldn't believe how long it took to put it all away.

After I'd finished I went back to the sitting room. and there they were. Curled up. Asleep on the sofa. L and the cat.

A lot happened when Violet was away. She was away a long time. And enough happened, frankly, for me not to mind how long.

First, of course, L left. I don't know why she left. You wouldn't believe how easy it was for her to leave. The place was mine. Most of the stuff in it was mine. All that stuff from the market. She just packed her bags and left. A couple of bags of clothes and make-up and stuff, and she left.

I didn't feel so good for a long time after she left. One of the things that didn't make me feel so good was the cat. I kept on thinking that she really must have not liked me, to leave the cat.

I put up this notice at work. Save the life of a cat. I didn't hear anything. I had this deputation. This group of people came to see me. In my office. I couldn't do it, they said. Who did I think I was? You can't just kill a cat, they said, just because you don't want it any more. So, I said. One of you is going to take it? Oh no. No one was going to take it. Not one of them was going to take it. They just felt they had to tell me. You can't kill a cat just because you don't want it any more.

In the end this friend of Jane's took it. He didn't want it that much either. Only Jane talked him into it. She was spending more and more time in Surrey now. Her and Ribbon. And she was seeing this man. And he agreed to take the cat.

Ribbon, she said, Jane said, had always liked the cat. The cat had often come visiting, and Ribbon had made friends with it. She liked it too. I didn't say anything about how I caught Ribbon throwing stones at it. I was too angry, frankly. All those times, I was thinking. All those times I was out in the garden, calling. All those times running up and down the street, calling, Tutti! Tutti! And all the time the cat was in the house. With Jane and Ribbon. With Violet. With Florrie too, I wouldn't be surprised.

It was good to be without it. The place felt clean without it. No more paw prints everywhere. No more dust and hair. No more litter and vomit. Above all no more food. No more every time I moved off to the dish for food. I threw the dish away. No more mewing and shaking and tail-trembling. It felt good. In the supermarket it felt really good. All those times in the supermarket, walking straight by the cat food section. You wouldn't believe how good that felt.

Then Violet came back.

Both flats had been done up. There was this South African in Florrie's old flat. He did something in films. He had all this editing stuff moved into the flat, and I could hear him doing his hoovering at odd times of the night. He told me when Violet was coming back. Her flat had been ready a long time.

She wasn't very well when she did come back. I expected her to go back to her old routine. Half past ten to the pub. Ten past three back. Eight o'clock to the pub eleven o'clock back. Tea at Barker's. Feathered hat and full gray coat. Only no. She didn't go out so much. The South African told me she wasn't so well. She wasn't eating, he told me. He used to make her meals and stuff, and take them down to her. But she wouldn't eat. Sometimes she wouldn't eat anything for days. He said.

One day this doctor rang my bell. It was at night. About eleven o'clock at night. I was in bed. When I went to the door it was this lady doctor, all bustling to get in.

I've come to see Mrs Rogers, she said.

You've come to the wrong place, I said. Mrs Rogers lives next door. How is she, by the way?

She looked at me like I shouldn't have asked. She looked at me all down her nose, and for a long time she didn't answer. And when she did answer it was a put down.

Mrs Roger's is very poorly, she said in this put down voice. That's why I've come to see her.

So, I thought when she'd gone. I suppose I look like some busybody neighbour. Someone who's always poking his nose in. Well, maybe I do. But at least I know where she lives. If I had a patient, at least I'd know where she lived.

The South African came to see me a few days later. He'd been talking to Violet, he said. And there was something he wanted to ask me. Did I have a cat? Did I have a cat called Tootsie? Only Violet kept on asking for this cat.

Tutti, I said. I used to have this cat called Tutti.

She calls it Tootsie, he said. And she'd like to see it again. She keeps on talking about it.

So I got the cat back. I got in touch with Jane, and she gave me her friend's number in Surrey. And when I called him he sounded relieved. The cat hadn't worked out. It hadn't got on with Ribbon, and he wasn't seeing so much of Jane these days anyway. He was happy enough for me to have it back. He got in touch with Jane, and she drove up from Surrey with it.

It spent most of its time at Violet's. The South African looked after it. I was going to give him some money to look after it, but he wouldn't take it. I kept the garden window shut. Sometimes the cat came and scratched at it but I didn't let it in. Sometimes it scratched and scratched. It just wouldn't go away. I got the earplugs out. Sometimes I let it in, but it was always soon scratching to get out again. I used to see it messing in the garden.

Violet didn't last much longer. The South African told me how she died. She didn't eat, and in the end she didn't drink, he said. She just lay in her bed till she died. I think she'd just had enough, he said. I think it was the fire, he said. I don't think she ever got over the fire. He said.

After she died I tried to get rid of the cat again. I offered it to the South African and to Jane but they didn't want it. I put up the notice in the office again, and I got a visit from the deputation again, but no one wanted it. I was going to take it to the vet, but in the end I didn't. You wouldn't believe how much it costs to take a cat to the vet.

And it didn't feel right somehow. I mean, don't get me wrong. I didn't like it. I still didn't like it. And it still didn't like me. It still wouldn't even let me pick it up. It was still dirty and messy. It was still throwing up. I had to go and buy a new blue plastic dish and every time I moved it ran for it. And there I was, every week, back at the pet food counter in the supermarket. I nearly took it to the vet often. But every time I nearly took it, I got to thinking how L had loved it. How it had purred and purred with her, and twined round her legs and head-butted her. And I thought of how Violet had liked it. I thought of Violet saying it's name wrong. That Tootsie, she said. She's a cat. I like that Tootsie. And every time I couldn't do it.

So there I was. With this cat.

Stuck. With this cat.

Encounters with Animals (2)

That was the bargain.

That, at least seemed to be the bargain. It was not a spoken bargain. Between the two of them, between Gregory Millom and Mr St George, very little was actually spoken.

In the day to day life of St Aelred's very little needed to be spoken. Master and pupil there, if the master did not actually teach the pupil, as Mr St George did not actually teach Gregory Millom, needed rarely even to see, let alone speak to, each other.

In the time they did spend together, although Mr St George did sometimes speak, it was less, Gregory Millom felt, in an attempt to communicate with him, certainly not to bargain with him, that to give voice to his own private emotions.

And if Mr St George had spoken, Gregory Millom would not actually have believed him. At twelve years old he was a seven year veteran of the St Aelred's system, and he had not, he told himself, got as far as he had without noticing that words were not always what they seemed. There was a gap, he had seen, between thought and word, between word and deed. It was quite usual, indeed it was a fact of life at St Aelred's, he had seen, to think one thing, say a second, and do a third. And Mr St George's words, such as they were, were neither more nor less to be relied on than any others.

Commerce between them was limited almost entirely to deeds.

And precisely because commerce between them was limited almost entirely to deeds, and because the deeds seemed to follow a regular pattern, it seemed to Gregory Millom that he could trust the deeds. That there was, in fact, a bargain between them, and the bargain was as follows: that Gregory Millom would do exactly as Mr St George wanted, that Gregory Millom would let Mr St George do exactly as he wanted, and that he, Mr St George, would love him.

That was the bargain.

They met every day at the top of St Robert's Tower. Mr St George had a room at the top of St Robert's Tower, and it was not easy for Gregory Millom to climb up to it, but every day, after Lunch, while everyone else was at Games, he would toil up the stairs, past the kitchens and the chapel, to Mr St George's room, high over the gatehouse, where Mr St George was waiting for him, and where, he knew, if he did exactly what Mr St George wanted, and let Mr St George do exactly what he wanted, Mr St George would love him.

It was the term of the callipers.

At the beginning of the previous term Gregory Millom had damaged his leg. In mid-September, the beginning of the Michaelmas term, he had twisted his right knee. He had fallen on the rugby field, and a loose scrum had formed around and over him, and his twisted knee had been trampled on and further twisted as the scrum passed. He had to be carried from the field.

His leg, Gregory Millom said, had never been the same since. Bandaged for a month, and rested, by the order of Dr Carter, the school doctor, it should have recovered by the end of October and had not. It remained, he said, stiff. He could neither run nor play Games, he said, without pain. His knee clicked audibly when he walked, and it tired him, he said, to stand.

At first daily, then weekly, Dr Carter had called Gregory Millom in to his surgery to inspect and manipulate him. In the end he pronounced himself baffled. At the beginning, he said, he had been inclined to doubt the injury. The knee, as far as he could see, had mended nicely. He had been inclined to suspect a little shirking, a little malingering, a spot of Oscillatio Plumbi, but he could not be sure. The audible click gave him pause. It was now November and the click had not gone away. There was nothing more, Dr Carter felt, that he could do.

He did not know, and Gregory Millom did not tell him, that the knee had clicked before the accident. Gregory Millom's knee had clicked for as long as he could remember. All the accident had done is make the click louder.

And the next term was the term of the callipers.

Twice before Christmas Dr Carter had driven Gregory Millom to a tall, honey-coloured house in the Royal Crescent in Bath, and had introduced him to a short man with hot hands and a striped waistcoat, a bald man with tufts of grey hair above his ears, and shaggy eyebrows and gold-rimmed half-moon glasses, who had talked to him about the house as he moved the leg this way and that way, and measured it against the other, noting the measurements in a thin leather-bound notebook with a thin gold pen.

It was a fine house, the man said. Didn't Gregory Millom think? One of the finest in the terrace. The staircase, he thought, was particularly fine. Had Gregory Millom seen the staircase?

He said the same thing on Gregory Millom's second visit. A very fine staircase, he said. A particularly fine example of a self-supporting staircase.

And after Christmas – a Christmas which had, as usual, driven all thought of St Aelred's out of his mind by reason of its very Christmasness, despite the fact that it was a smaller and quieter Christmas this year, and his Grandmother, who usually spent it with them, this year, for some reason, had stayed away – after Christmas, back at St Aelred's for the Easter term, he had forgotten all about his knee. It came as a surprise when he heard his name called out in Assembly and he was told that Dr Carter had arranged for Mr St George to drive him to Bath the next afternoon for his third visit.

And on the third visit the callipers were fitted, which was even more of a surprise.

The callipers fitted from thigh to ankle. They ran from a circle of padded leather at the top to the heel of Gregory Millom's shoe at the bottom. As the man cut two small holes in the heel of his shoe to accommodate the callipers he talked about the house.

I don't know if you noticed it, he said. But the self-supporting staircase is particularly fine.

On the way back to St Aelred's, sitting in the front seat of Mr St George's car, sitting next to Mr St George, Gregory Millom did not know what to think. His callipers, hinged at the knee so that he could sit down, chaffed his thigh. He sat quiet in his seat, and he must have looked very glum, because after thirty minutes or so, Mr St George parked the car in a lay-by outside Shepton Mallet, and reached across and held his hand.

It was a long time since someone had held Gregory Millom's hand. His Grandmother had held his hand. Often when they sat together, or went on walks together, or took the bus together, she would hold his hand. If they were sitting next to each other she would take his hand in both of her hands, and stroke it. Sometimes she would lift his hand to her mouth and kiss it. Sometimes he would lift her hand to his mouth and kiss it. He had not seen his Grandmother for a long time.

His Grandmother was ill.

His Grandmother, his mother and father had told him in the car on the way back to St Aelred's after Christmas, was very ill. His Grandmother was in hospital in Bournemouth. His Grandmother had missed Christmas because she was in hospital in Bournemouth.

He held Mr St George's hand.

Mr St George took his hand in both of his hands and stroked it.

He lifted Mr St George's hand to his mouth and kissed it.

Soon afterwards Mr St George released his hand, put his arm round his shoulder, and pulled him towards him. Mr St George held his face between his hands for a long time and looked at him. Then Mr St George kissed him.

Gregory Millom loved his Grandmother.

Mr St George was a TT. A Temporary Teacher. The latest in a long succession. It was the custom at St Aelred's to employ TTs. Only last year Mr St George, like the other TTs, had been at school himself. At the end of last year Mr St George had left Hales, due to go up at the beginning of the next to Oxford. He was spending the intervening time, a year was the limit for TTs, working at St Aelred's.

Mr St George had made, before the kiss, little impact on Gregory Millom's life at St Aelred's. TTs didn't. TTs taught only the youngest pupils, and in his seven years at the school, working his way up from year to year to his present position under Mr Lomax himself, in the scholarship class, Gregory Millom had seen as many TTs come and go. He had known no more than the names of most of them. If it had not been for Gregory Millom's leg, and the fact that Mr St George was free that afternoon while Dr Carter was not – there was a match with All Hallows, Dr Carter was a hearty cheerer at all school fixtures, Mr St George cared nothing for football – Mr St George would not have been detailed to drive Gregory Millom into Bath, and would have remained no more for Gregory Millom than what he had always been, a distant figure with a fine-sounding name. And, kissless, Gregory Millom's life would have continued in its former track.

As it was, the kiss changed things. The kiss, Gregory Millom found when, the next day after lunch, after a night and a morning of wondering what he should do next, he toiled in his callipers up the stairs to Mr St George's room over the gatehouse, the kiss had changed things.

The kiss, he found when he knocked on Mr St George's door, and saw in Mr St George's startled eyes as he looked up from his desk, that he was not, as Gregory Millom half expected, angry with him, that he was rather, he seemed to be at least, if only at the beginning, what Gregory Millom had expected that he, Gregory Millom, was supposed to be, what teachers, even TTs, were not supposed to be, anxious, that is, and fidgety and even a little afraid, the kiss, he found, when they had made their explanations – again without words, Gregory Millom had tried to speak but was so disturbed by the fact that Mr St George obviously found his presence disturbing that he could think of nothing to say, and Mr St George, too, had had trouble speaking – the kiss was the first of many.

The kiss, and all the subsequent kisses, as he found over the next few days and weeks, when every day after lunch, when everyone else was at Games, he toiled up the stairs past the kitchens and chapel to Mr St George's room, to Mr St George's arms, in St Robert's Tower, meant there was a bargain between them.

And the bargain meant that he was loved. It was not the sort of love he was used to. The sort of love he was used to was his Grandmother's, and, though it was similarly without words – it consisted mainly of hand holding, and smiles, and friendly company – it was easier to navigate. There was no risk in it. There was no furtiveness. There was no knowing that no one else would understand, no not speaking to each other outside Mr St George's room, no avoiding each other's eyes in Assembly, no not even looking at each other when they passed in the corridor. Above all there were no conditions. There was no doing everything Mr St George wanted, there was no letting Mr St George do everything he wanted. His Grandmother's love was not like Mr St George's. His Grandmother's love was a gift.

Mr St George's love was a bargain.

But it was love at least, and at St Aelred's, Gregory Millom felt, love, even silent, bargaining love, was something he wanted.

And Mr St George's requirements were not arduous.

They were to undress him, and be undressed by him. To hold him, and be held by him. To embrace him, and have his embraces enthusiastically returned. It was not difficult.

It was only, at times, a bit odd.

When Mr St George spoke it was a bit odd. Because when Mr St George spoke it was less, Gregory Millom felt, Gregory Millom had worked out, to talk to him, Gregory Millom, than to himself, less to communicate than to give voice to his own private emotions. Mr St George's words could, Gregory Millom felt, make sense only to Mr St George. They certainly, or rather not the words, but the context in which Mr St George spoke them, made no sense to Gregory Millom.

Because Mr St George, while doing all the things he wanted to Gregory Millom, while having Gregory Millom do all the things he wanted to him, said, all the time he was doing it, the same thing over and over, sometimes under his breath, sometimes out loud, but always the same, over and over. Do it to me, he said. Do it to me, he said, kissing Gregory Millom, embracing Gregory Millom. Do it to me, he said. And that, to Gregory Millom, was a bit odd. It was after all, wasn't it? Mr St George who was doing all these things to him.

But this was just a bit odd. Merely a bit odd. A bit odd is not difficult. This was just part of the bargain. This was just something Mr St George wanted. And all Gregory Millom had to do was everything Mr St George wanted, let Mr St George do everything he wanted, and Mr St George would love him.

Gregory Millom saw the hare on the day he heard his

Grandmother had died. His mother wrote to him, and he took the letter to the lavatories to read it. The lavatories were the only place at St Aelred's where you could be private, and he read all his letters there. It was part of the St Aelred's system.

His Grandmother had died, his mother wrote to him, in her hospital in Bournemouth. His Grandmother, his mother wrote, had been ill for a very long time. Nothing less than being very ill would, his mother knew he knew, have kept his Grandmother away from home at Christmas. His Grandmother had died quietly and without pain. She had simply fallen asleep one night, and not woken up in the morning. His Grandmother, he was to remember, had loved him very much. Almost the last words his Grandmother had spoken before she fell asleep that last night were to ask to be remembered to him. Tell him, his Grandmother had said, that I love him.

That afternoon, after lunch, when everyone else was at Games, he did not climb the staircase to Mr St George's room. He went for a walk instead. He toiled in his callipers out through the gate, out under St Robert's Tower over the gate-house, out over roads and fields. He and his Grandmother had often gone for walks together. His Grandmother had loved to walk. His Grandmother would hold his hand, and they would walk and walk and walk. He walked until he came to the bottom of St Aelred's Hill, and slowly, awkwardly because of the callipers, climbed it. At the top of St Aelred's Hill was Old St Aelred's, a ruined church, a stand of wall, an arch, a locked chancel inches deep, St Aelred's lore had it, in dead flies, a tumbled tower, some tumbled gravestones.

Among the gravestones he saw the hare.

The hare was small, crouched in a tussock of grass among the gravestones, and he nearly trod on it.

The hare was small and thin, crouched in its tussock of grass, and when he leaned over to look closer at it, standing still and breathing low so as not to startle it, surprised that he had not already startled it, he saw that it had no eyes. It had never had any eyes. Over its eye sockets, where its eyes should have been, was a layer of skin. And it was startled. It was so startled that all it could do was sit in its tussock of grass and pant.

The hare was very thin. Gregory Millom could see its ribs moving under its skin as it panted. The hare was so thin that he could see its skin move over its ribs like canvas over railings. He leaned over it, and was going to bend down and touch it when he saw that another shadow was leaning over him.

The shadow leaned over him and the hare till it covered them both, and, slowly, awkwardly because of the callipers, Gregory Millom turned to find Mr St George standing over him.